Way of the Ghosts

A Collection of 20 Short Stories

By Jesse Calnan

First Edition 2023

Library and Archives Canada
ISBN 978-1-998245-01-7 (Paperback)

Edited by Danielle L'Ami
Cover design by Kabrena L. Robinson
Published by Eva-Michelle & Family Publishing
www.evamichelleandfamily.com

Table of Contents

RESPECT THE DEAD

A man named Bob Roberts sat at the cemetery every day shoveling holes and drinking beer. Some days, Bob would be working on the gardens. He liked doing the gardens, it was more fun than digging someone's final home, and of course, it was easier on the body. Overall, he didn't mind working hard; he loved his job at the cemetery, but he had been there since he was a young lad getting out of juvie. After twenty years, he was sick of the poor pay, and he heard that robbing graves paid better.

There was a wealthy man named William Cuddy. Bob was digging the man's grave with a six-pack beside him and a smoke in his mouth.

His good friend Todd was next to him, to help with the digging.

Todd polished off a can of beer, and then he said to Bob, "You know, rumour has it this old coot believed he could take everything with him. I'm sure he's going to be dressed to the hilts full of jewelry. He might even have some of his fortune in there with him."

"You saying what I think you're saying?" Bob replied.

"I've got it all planned out, buddy. This coot's coming in here tomorrow afternoon, right? So, let's come back here and get him tomorrow night."

"Well, I don't think he'll miss anything, and he certainly won't even know we took a thing." Then the two gravediggers laughed, opened another beer, toasted each other with their drinks, and drank away.

That night, when Bob went to sleep, he could hear some creaking through his house. As he was the only one that lived there, he found it strange, and he didn't know the place to have rats or mice. But as he moved his head, he saw what looked like a flash of green light coming toward him. It felt like a huge gust.

Then, before it knocked him out, he saw, Mr. Cuddy's face in the glowing light. An evil growl came from the face. "That's my gold," he said and followed with a laugh.

Bob woke up the next morning feeling terrible. He noticed he had wet the bed. He didn't think he was that drunk. Then he remembered what he thought was a strange hallucination. He didn't take it as a warning, instead, he took it as more inspiration to rob the grave. He took it as his confirmation that there would be gold there and it would be worth their while to take.

He went off to work that morning and drove around the graveyard on a buggy. He arrived at a plot to dig just atop of the hill from where Mr. Cuddy was being buried. There was a large crowd there, obviously of the high society type. Luxury suits, a Cadillac hearse, and all the women had beautiful jewelry along with their expensive dresses.

This made Bob even angrier. He didn't have anything in his life except a shovel, some beer, and a gun under his bed. Those were the possessions he most enjoyed, but watching this man have everything made Bob furious. He had lots of money, plenty of friends, a wife, and kids;

everything you could ask for. This made his mind completely made up.

Maybe I could have a little piece of the pie for a change, he thought.

He looked over to Todd at the next hole and he called his name, "Let's get that S.O.B."

Todd gave him a thumbs-up and a smile. "Meet you here at midnight?"

"You got it, buddy."

That night they rode their bikes down to the graveyard. Each of them brought a backpack and a few burlap sacks to carry the goods they would steal. They started digging up what they filled in that day. But since they had known they would be back that night they decided not to pack it down or put the hard ground back in. The two dug the dirt from the grave for an hour and a half.

After their hard work, Todd hit Mr. Cuddy's solid oak coffin with his shovel. They dusted off the last bit of dirt and then broke open part of the casket. When they looked in, they noticed he wasn't wearing a chain. When they got the rest of the casket open, they saw no ring, watches, or anything of value.

Next, Todd looked through the dead man's pocket. That is when Todd felt the cold dead grip of a corpse grabbing his arm. He froze completely, in temperature and stiffness. The corpse's eyes were wide open. Bob fell back onto the ground and watched the horrid creature grab his friend.

The corpse dropped back into the casket, but the spirit of the man came out, a dreaded-looking green face surrounded by glowing green flames.

The horrible ghost rose to the top of the grave and gave a dreaded yell, "You should have not come here." Then the dirt started flying down on them. They pulled themselves up to the surface as quickly as they could, but the demon attached himself to Todd and started sucking the life out of him. He screamed in terror. Bob ran through the cemetery as quickly as he could before an owl came at him. The owl grew dark then he grew to a six-foot-tall beast with a ten-foot wingspan. He gusted Bob backward, smashing over a gravestone awakening more ghosts. Bob jumped up. He started running, but he could feel the demons grabbing him. He was getting cold and quickly losing energy. He managed to keep running and get to his bike, but as he jumped on it, he could see

Todd being pushed into the opened grave by the ghost of William Cuddy. The demons all left Bob's side, heading for the grave. He then noticed a flashing light on Cuddy's grave, which was quickly filled with loose dirt encasing Todd's body in the grave.

Bob started to ride his bike again and felt himself getting away until he felt the spirits stop him almost dead in his tracks.

William Cuddy's evil green spirit appeared in front of him. "You have forsaken your role as caretaker and have awoken the spirits that were once settled. You sir will rot in hell forever."

Right after William Cuddy's ghost finished speaking, a hand came from under Bob ripping him off his bike and sucking him under the ground, leaving the bike behind.

The next morning, the foreman of the cemetery was doing his inspection. He had seen a bottle of whiskey and a bike sitting beside the newly planted grave. When he got to the plot and read it he saw that it was the stone of William Cuddy. He thought it was very strange as he expected someone to rob the millionaire, but it didn't look like it had even been touched.

He figured it was a drunken relative who had left the bottle, but then he noticed the broken headstone and figured it was an angry drunken relative.

He started to walk away until he noticed another bike sitting on top of a grave. The stone had a large smiley face, and it read, "Be happy with whatever you got."

When the foreman started walking back, one of the gardeners came up and said "Hey, have you seen Todd or Bob today? They are supposed to be helping me."

"No, haven't seen them all day." Answered his boss. He then looked at his watch and saw it was already quarter to eleven. He looked up and muttered to himself. "Damn drunks, and they want a raise, yeah right."

AN UNFORTUNATE ACCIDENT

A ninety-year-old man had lived in the same house his whole life. His name was Jerry; he had a twenty-year-old neighbour that lived next to him, and they were good friends.

The young man's name was Mason; Jerry called him Martin or Mart, most of the time. He was bad with names. Mason would come over almost every night, they would sit outside drinking a beer in the summer, or in the winter they sat inside drinking and enjoying the hockey game.

Jerry used to complain about the way the world was sometimes. Everything had changed drastically since he was a boy. The thing he hated the most about the change in the neighbourhood was an arrogant mechanic that had a business on the other side of him. Jerry had a big backyard that was home to a beautiful vegetable garden. The whole block was like that there was even a community greenhouse next door. That all changed when Rick the auto mechanic bought the next lot over and turned the yard into a parking lot for his shop. He had plans that he wanted to do the same thing to Jerry's property.

Jerry always said, "That jerk will never get my property. I swear to God I'll blow his brains out before that happens if it's the last thing I do." Jerry was just a short man with a high voice and crooked teeth, so it was funny when he complained like that.

Jerry didn't quite own the house. His brother, who was the owner, had just passed away, and Jerry did not have the ownership yet, so, he couldn't name Mason as the beneficiary of the house like he wanted to.

Mason used to cut the grass for the jerk mechanic, until one time, while he was getting a quote Rick said, "Maybe once I have Jerry's place I'll rent it to you, and you can help fill in the garden." Mason never got work done there again.

That winter, Mason got a job working nights and he couldn't see Jerry quite as much. Eventually, the loneliness got to Jerry, and he died months after Mason took the job.

Mason was very sad his best friend was dead. Now, he would be just as lonely as Jerry. The house was put up for sale and although Mason tried saving enough to buy it, he didn't have $50,000 for a down payment, unlike Rick. Rick had been talking to the bank and soon would be able to buy the house within a matter of days.

One night, Rick was at his shop clearing out his safe, he put $50,000 in a small shaving bag he had strapped in his coat. It was dark, cold, and windy that night. He planned to take the money home with him and go to the bank early the next morning. But just as he was about to leave, the power went out in the neighbourhood.

At the same time, Mason was sitting in his attic watching a hockey game. When the power went out, his best friend's face appeared in front of him in a shining blue light.

All he said was, "That S.O.B isn't getting my house; I told you what the last thing I was going to do was."

Then he disappeared and the lights went back on in every place, except for Rick's. Rick started to leave but the wind and snow started blowing at him hard. He couldn't see anything with his parking lot being pitch black from the power outage. As he got to his truck a bunch of snow came off the roof blowing at him knocking him to the ground and loosening his money bag.

Rick got back in the truck. The whole time he drove, his truck was shaking from the wind. He finally got to his beautiful home. He sat by his fireplace and poured a fine glass of bourbon. Then, he made sure his gun was sitting on his wall with a bullet in it. He had one in his living room and bedroom in case someone ever tried to invade his home. As he sat there, he watched the snow come down from his window. Then suddenly, he saw a large chunk of wood drop in front of his door shaking his house. His gun dropped from the fireplace pointing right at him. He got up to look.

Then he said to himself, after inspection, "That's a lucky mistake I made; I never put it on safety." Then he decided to go to bed for the night.

After getting comfortable in his bed to sleep, the

storm became even worse. His window blasted open, causing the shattered glass to fall all over him. He stood up with the freezing wind coming at him, covered in glass. He was freezing cold only this cold seemed like a different kind of cold than the weather. While he stood there frightened, a large chunk of a tree came smashing through the ceiling. He screamed, then he felt a great gust push him back.

While he was falling backwards, Jerry's face appeared, and he said "You think you're cute? I'm a hell of a lot cuter." As Rick fell back once more, he tried to grab onto whatever he could. He grabbed onto his rifle; it came down barrel first at him. But as it came down it slipped on his finger pulling the trigger allowing Jerry to do the last thing he said he would ever do.

The next morning, Mason stepped out his back door and saw a shaving bag with fifty-thousand dollars in it. He ran inside and hid in the most secret part of the house. He called the bank and told them he got his inheritance from a friend. The police questioned him once about the money and the death of Rick, but there was too much evidence that Rick committed suicide, accidental or not.

So, there was no further investigation.

After Mason bought the house, he turned it into a garden shop. He put a greenhouse in one corner of the yard and made the rest a garden. He also put a flower shop inside the antique-style parlour that greeted the door.

THE PARK OF HELL

A man left a New York City bar at two a.m. Usually, the street was a hot ticket, but he noticed there was no one out except for an ambulance driving in the far distance that turned the corner and was gone. Rex Fadden was the man's name. He looked around and found it very peculiar that he was the only one on the street. Even after Reggie's bar closed for the night, nobody came out, only him.

Rex tried to get in his car, but it wouldn't open for him; probably for the best considering he had had a couple of drinks. He staggered down the street and still no people. He walked down a dark alley and for a while there was nobody. Then he walked a little farther and saw a light with people underneath. He went to speak to these men, but he couldn't understand a word they were saying, nothing but drunken mutters.

After failing to strike up a conversation with them, he kept walking down the alley and there he saw many people in horrid shapes.

There was a woman in ragged old clothes and long dirty mangled hair screaming out of control with a cat in her hand and two bums sitting on the ground soaked in whiskey who looked half dead. He walked further on and saw more haggard people. Everyone was disgusting including a man with a ripped shirt, with a skinny chest popping out. He had a scar across his eyes, both of which were white, and he started coming towards Rex. Rex punched the man, but his punch went right through him. Surprisingly, he felt a warmth of heat go through him. The man kept walking away, groaning like a zombie.

Rex kept walking down the dark miserable street with treacherous mongrels all around him. As he walked, his clothes started to become tattered as well. He started to become malnourished extremely quickly.

He began to feel terrible inside. As he kept walking, he saw light. When he got to the light, he saw luxury ballrooms filled with tremendous food and beautiful people in great outfits. The people there were having the time of their lives. He went to walk into one of the rooms, but he could not open the door. He kept walking down the road, but it became dark and dreary again. After walking through the hell hole for hours, he walked into an opening, it was the great park.

At first, it looked quiet. Again, it seemed like he was on his own in a ghost town. He walked down a large stairway and it seemed much larger than he remembered; it started to darken even more, which he didn't think was even possible.

As he went down farther through the pitch blackness, the last hour of his life flashed before his eyes. He could see himself at Reggie's bar. He was drinking, talking big, making racist comments, and hitting on women with his wife at home. He didn't know why it flashed before him. Since that good memory, he had seen nothing but a living hell, maybe that was why. The last part of the memory showed him on the ground covered in his own vomit. After the image ended, he stepped a little further down the stairs. He was then ripped to the ground and was surrounded by the tattered misfits he had seen before, but this time they looked like demons. They grabbed him, ripping at his soul.

As he lay there on the ground getting torn apart, the beast appeared. The Devil moved the demons out of its way and stood in front of him.
Lucifer said, "For the way you have lived, the way treated your wife, the way you cheated people, your lack of empathy, selfishness, and disrespect has given me the right to your soul." Then the Devil flew into Rex's body where he let out a horrid scream. The demons got on top of him and did their evil magic.

As Rex lay there becoming a demon, he wished he respected life just a little bit more...

THE HAUNTED PLANT

Sam Tucker worked at a car factory, Common Engines, for twenty years. The giant factory grounds had been there for over sixty years. Whatever you can imagine, likely happened at the factory. In the earlier days of the factory being open, there were wild parties every Friday night, people got into fights, and one man was even stabbed to death. In another incident, a man was so sick of his boss that he shot him in the chest.

The factory had four separate buildings within it. Each one was named after a letter. B stood for bodywork, C for chassis, and D to keep the letters in alphabetical order. Lastly, the fourth building, although you would think it would be Building A, was actually Building S; it had not been used in over thirty years. Most of the men and women who had died at the factory lost their lives in building S. After the first few died, strange accidents started happening, and the machinery started malfunctioning. Many employees became scared saying the building was haunted. Then one day, another man died in a very strange manner; they found him frozen to death in a corner with a mop; he died of hypothermia. The coroner said that this was the strangest thing he had ever seen since it had been a warm day at the time of his death. That was the last incident, from then on, they shut it down and made it into a storage building. Nobody would go into building S too often anymore, but if they did, they made sure it was quick, and no one ever went alone.

Over the last ten years of Sam working at the factory most of the production had been shut down and three thousand people had been laid off. Only a few hundred kept their jobs for maintenance because there was still some money left over to spend from the government's bailout.

During Sam's last ten years of working through

the shutdown he spent most of his time driving a cart and exploring the factory, but there was one place he never entered, building S.

The factory started growing dark and dreary over the last ten years. Some days, he would experience the scariest chills he ever felt. Like when he would go through empty offices. There was one office that spooked him the most. It was on the second floor where the executive offices were located.

It was a big office room with many desks in an open space. The executive offices also had private offices attached to them. Sam was walking through them one day, not minding his own business, when he went to open one of the doors. When he touched the handle, it shocked him and he fell backwards. Then the door opened. When it creaked open, a shining light flashed through before the door slammed shut. Sam got up and ran out of the offices and jumped on his buggy as quickly as he could.

He didn't believe his eyes. He had always heard the place was haunted, but he never believed it. He had also felt weird feelings before, but he ignored them. Now he believed.

He didn't want to tell anyone, because he didn't want to look like a crazy believer that everyone laughed about.

During the shutdown, Sam had seen some other spooky things, but he had gotten used to the fact that the place was haunted. It never bothered him anymore. Except for one time when he was walking up a metal mezzanine stairwell and the face of a woman flew at him knocking him down the stairs right onto his arse. He got a few months off after that. He wanted to say it was a ghost, but he knew he wouldn't have gotten workmen's compensation with that kind of explanation. When he came back, he was extra careful. He didn't go into any dark hidden spots anymore, even though he loved hiding in those places, it was too risky. He also tried to avoid using any stairs the best he could. He especially avoided building S, along with everyone else. The building stayed unused during the shutdown. The place must have been completely terrifying.

After nine years the factory got another bailout. This time it was for ten billion dollars. It was given to them to reopen the plant. There was a contractor that was always on CM property, Jon

Ryerson Construction Company. He had been there for the last year of the shutdown. Sam was transferred to work for the contractor. He found the construction work easy, but harder than working on the CE line or travelling for hours, which he still got to do a lot of.

His main job working for them was doing cleanup; he swept a lot of stuff. After that, he got into demolishing washrooms. One day they were taking apart stalls in a woman's facility. Rumour had it that a woman had overdosed in there. It was the same washroom that was up the stairs that Sam had once fallen from.

He smashed a stall door off with a crowbar. It took three hits from the crowbar, then when it came loose, a wicked scream let out. The same face of the woman he had seen before appeared before him, letting out the same wretched sound. Sam fell back against another stall and the ghost blew him back knocking all the stalls down. One of his co-workers Cory came in. Cory had seen the flashing light and when he walked in, he even blew back with the ghostly gust.

They both screamed but the ghost disappeared just before the foreman walked in.

The foreman saw Sam lying on the ground in the messy washroom, one of the toilets spraying water.

"What the hell is going on here?" the foreman asked.

"A ghost!" Cory yelled.

"Don't tell me you guys believe in that crap? Clean this mess up, then I want you two to help a few guys to clean an office."

The foreman was sending Cory and Sam up to the same office Sam had tried to enter before but was stopped by the ghost. After they cleaned up the big mess, the two of them drove to the office on a golf cart.

The whole time, Cory was going on and on about the ghost. Saying things like, "We don't have to put up with that crap" or "I'm outta here, man." He kept repeating these things, but he really didn't seem to have any intentions of going home.

The guys drove up to the elevator. When Sam clicked the button, the panel started flashing like crazy, then a long weary beep lingered as the door opened. They got on; Cory was terrified. Sam had gotten quite used to the ghosts, but he was still quite scared to go to the dreaded office again.

When they got to the hallway in front of the office, they noticed a dumpster full of very valuable office supplies including books, chairs, tables, pens, binders, and even a bible. When they got a little farther down the hall, they saw a group of people gathered around. They were all watching as a man on a stretcher being taken past them. As soon as Sam saw someone, he immediately asked what had happened. A man told him that a carpenter's apprentice was finishing clearing an office and he dropped dead at the site.

The man pointed out the office, but Sam already knew where it happened. People were claiming it was a ghost, but the bosses all said they were nuts. Then the foreman told Cory and Sam that they would be working in building S tomorrow.

Sam's heart sank. He said, "We can't!"

"Why not? Are you scared of ghosts?"

Sam made a fist. He felt like punching his boss, but he held back. Then the boss told him, "If you're not here tomorrow, you're fired. And release that fist, we all know you're not going to use It." Then they both turned separate ways and walked to their carts.

When they got back to the cart Cory said, "Hell, with all that's happened, I'm not coming in tomorrow." Sam just kind of looked at him and shook his head knowing he was full of it."

The next day, Sam showed up. He waited for Cory for fifteen minutes; he started to think he was for real. Then, sure enough, Cory showed up. He was usually late anyway.

The foreman came up to them and told them they had to do some washroom demos in building S.

Sam and Cory already knew this, and they had dreaded it all night, but they drove over and got over the fear. They took a strange way to get there because the garage doors didn't even work. There was a tunnel from building B going over to the haunted warehouse. They drove to the far end of building B and entered the tunnel. The first part was as clean as the rest of the building. Once they turned the corner, that changed. It became dark and they couldn't see ahead of themselves. They turned on their headlamps and their lanterns. They soon saw that they were driving into a giant spider web across the entire tunnel. They kept driving through the dark hall until they entered the warehouse. The two workers were both terrified; they could hear rats; they even saw one run by.

 The light shined into the building from the broken windows and old ceiling glass. It vaguely lit a small part of the building but most of it remained dark. They made their way through the dirty, awful, abandoned building. As they walked up the stairs to the washroom, it was almost complete darkness, so they shone a light. The whole time they were in there, the temperature was much below normal. Despite this, they finished their work for the day; it surprisingly went well.

As they were walking back to the cart, Sam saw a small flag banner that said CE 1960 building S. He needed to have it. After all the legendary tales, he was the first one in there for 30 years. He would be a legend himself with that flag. So, he grabbed the flag, folded it up, and snuck it into his waistline. He felt a chill down his leg as he did that.

The two men drove out of building S without any hauntings, and Sam had a memento. They drove through building B and over to C. As they entered, they both got a great chill. Sam wondered if he made a mistake by taking the flag. He tried not to think about it until he started driving past the first production line that was starting to be used.

In the middle of the factory, the cart they were on burst into flames. Sam and Cory both sat there burning to a crisp while spirits came from throughout the factory holding the flag that Sam had taken. They watched the shining flag before their dying eyes.

The fire from the cart spread onto the line and wall. Four spirits came from the ground and turned into powerful flames. Each of them headed in a different direction, spreading the blaze across the entire ground of the plant. Rapidly every building caught fire. Until they burned down to a complete crisp of ashes and soot. Some people made it out alive but very few did due to the dimwitted security guards not letting people leave without checking them. They were too busy doing that to notice the flames surrounding them.

A week after the destructive fire, the president of CE announced they would get a fifty-billion-dollar bailout to rebuild the plant.

PIRATES OF THE DEAD

The water had been calm and the sun had been shining greatly, but somehow, there was a storm on a beautiful day. The storm had been cast for over a week, but not a cloud was in sight. If you were anywhere else in the ocean, you would most likely say it was a sailor's delight. The waters of Smokey Bay had endured one of the worst storms it had ever dealt with.

The storm first struck with a cannonball soaring over the water blasting a hole in a proud ship. The sailors on the ship readied their guns and put themselves into position. Unfortunately, after the pirates had boarded, there was nothing the sailors could do. It was the worst pirate attack to happen in ages. Every one of the sailors on that ship was taken to Davey Jones' locker in the remains of a burning wreck. No survivors were left to tell the tale. The pirates made sure they shot down any man who tried to swim for his life.

Attacks went on like this all through the week, boats sunken or found destroyed with no survivors. It didn't matter the size of the ship or who was on it. Fishermen had been reported missing, cruise vessels sunken down, as well as cargo ships and navy carriers. The naval troops and freight sailors put up good fights, but the pirates were better.

The wildest thing about these attacks was the valuables that were being found on the remains of the ships, beautiful jewelry, cash, and crates of many desires. The one thing that was taken from every ship was the weapons. It seemed that these pirates only cared about destruction.

A lot of people were trying to say the weather caused the shipwrecks, even though the sky had been perfect. Captain Robert Gamble knew that the weather had nothing to do with the storm. He had faced pirates before but from what he was hearing, it seemed like he had never seen anything like this.

Robert Gamble was the captain of his ship, the SS. Poker Queen. One day, he had a delivery to make across the Atlantic Ocean it was scheduled to take just over a week to get there. He really didn't want to make the journey with what he knew to be pirate trouble, but the delivery needed to be made on time and any other route would take too long travelling along the shorelines.

Robert strapped his men properly; every man held a navy Colt and a sawed-off shotgun. He had more than enough rifles for everyone stacked all through the boat in the most convenient spots if needed quickly. Robert even made a trade with a friend; he gave some extra goods he had acquired over the years in exchange for two canons. He wanted to make damn sure that he was prepared for whatever storm would be coming his way.

Don Hodgson was Roberts' first mate. The two first met in the Navy and became great friends after saving each other's lives from time to time. After the navy, Robert got his own business and bought his own ship. The first person he asked to join him was Don, and he quickly accepted the offer. They had been in business for over ten years together. They had faced many storms and awful pirates in their time, both in the navy and shipping.

Before the crew set out, Robert stood on the dock and told every single one of his men as they got on the boat. "Be prepared for anything, if not, turn around now." Every man got on the ship not questioning Robert at all. They all knew there would be an awful storm even if it was sunny out.

After the boat was loaded and the men got on, the ship set sail. They sailed for the entire day and the weather was fine, so they continued right through the night, changing shifts at midnight. The crew made good pace through the night into the next afternoon, and they didn't see any other ships in sight. But after another day of sailing the open blue, a lightning bolt came from out of nowhere.

The beautiful weather soon changed to a dark night sky. Thunder started booming and lightning flashed all around them. Out of nowhere, three ships came sailing right toward them from different directions. Each ship was made from weathered wood, half dilapidated, and falling apart. The ships had traditional black flags, with a skull and cross bones on each one. There were ugly, fleshless men with no teeth or eyes riding on the deck of the approaching vessels.

The strange pirates stood at the front of the boats, wielding swords and guns of different varieties. As they got closer, cannons kept going off. Robert Gamble set off the alarm to let everyone know that they were under attack; the cannons were more than enough warning. Every sailor grabbed a rifle and ensured all their guns were ready and loaded.

Robert sent his first mate, Don, to one of his cannons while he went to the other leaving a crewman to steer the ship. Although the man was experienced in evading pirates, this was the biggest test he had faced working on the SS. Poker Queen.

Robert and Don both started firing the cannons back at the pirates while they gave commands to the sailors. The ships kept getting closer and bombs blasted from every direction. As the ships closed in on one another, the weather kept getting worse. Once they got in close range, gunshots started being exchanged. Many pirates were being shot in fatal spots, but they weren't going down, they just kept firing. Men on the SS. Poker Queen, however, were not as lucky. Robert Gamble was quickly losing men. The ship had taken a blast on each side, and with more coming, the boat was quickly being destroyed. Robert knew it would be going under soon. His side had started to sink. He called out a warning to his men and they ran over to where Don was. He gathered whomever he could; he had a plan.

Once he arrived at Don's side, he let him know what he wanted to do. As the ship was sinking, he grabbed a rope ladder and swung it onto the pirate's ship. The pirate's ship also had a cannon blast in the side, but it wasn't sinking quite as quickly as his was. He told them when they got on the ship to fire at everything they saw. Men started climbing the ladder while firing their weapons. Robert and his crew started getting onto the pirate's ship and started shooting wildly.

Two dozen men made it onto the ship and survived the initial attack. Robert pulled out a jar of moonshine then lit it and threw it at the pirates. But these were not your ordinary pirates; they were the walking dead. But despite this, the flames slowly took their life away. The ship started growing in flames. Roberts's men spread across the ship, shooting at the zombie pirates, but the bullets couldn't stop them. Don made a torch out of a metal rod. He took two cloths, wrapping one around his hand to keep it cool, the other, he lit with his Zippo. He went around the ship lighting everything he saw on fire, but the pirates still came at them firing their guns while they melted away.

After burning most of the first pirate ship, they boarded the next one over. Robert started to lose his men again on that ship. Once they got on, they continued firing their guns even though it didn't affect the zombies, but the fire did. Robert made a torch as Don had, and they both waved the flames towards the pirates. He used the fire to back them up, then he threw it at them. The beasts started coming towards him as they melted into a pile of slime. One of the pirates came running at him; he was nothing more than a burning skeleton. Yielding a sword, the zombie pirate ran at Robert. Robert fired his gun, but it didn't work on the walking corpse. He changed his tactics and sliced at him with the bayonet on his gun until Don tackled the zombie to the ground. When Don took him down, his first mate screamed as he burned into a crisp of ashes. Robert was mortified watching his best friend burn into a pile of flames, dying to save his life. He went cold for a minute then he ran on instinct.

He yelled, "Boys get their cannon working and work on the other pirate ship. Let's take 'er down and hop a dingy."

The men started firing the canon at the other ship while Robert continued to burn the other half of the ship. They only had a few minutes before the whole thing went down. As Robert's men started firing canons at the other ship, those pirates started boarding their ship. Both ships started to sink; the Zombie pirates that made it aboard started devouring the sailors. Every one of Robert's men was dying in front of him; the whole boat started to burn. The flames pushed him to the edge of the ship where he noticed a lifeboat. He cut the rope and jumped aboard. The giant wreck of four boats started collapsing all around him. He paddled the fastest he ever had. He didn't think he was going to make it, pieces of burned wood were flying all around him.

Somehow, he managed to get out of the wreckage. The storm ended up blowing him far from the drowning ships. For miles, he saw the flames bursting atop the water. The storm lasted for what seemed like a lifetime. The winds from the storm continued to carry him away through the wild ocean. Even after the shipwreck, he just stayed in the lifeboat, floating for his life. He was starving and exhausted; he was also going mad. Finally, after several days at sea, and almost starving to death, he landed on a beach. When the lifeboat made its final drift to shore, he was half asleep when he noticed he was no longer on the water. He climbed out of the lifeboat and dropped to his stomach. He started crawling on the beach until a woman noticed him.

She screamed, "Help!" A lifeguard came running over along with a few other people. A crowd gathered around him.

The lifeguard got him to the nearest doctor very quickly. When Robert Gamble became alert, he asked the doctor where the hell he was. He found out he had made it to his destination, but he still came up short. He had lost his men, his ship, and his complete livelihood. Now he was many days from his home with no transportation and no money. The doctor asked him if he remembered what had happened to him and if there had been a storm.

Robert told the doctor, "There was a storm, all right, the worst group of pirates I've ever seen. Zombie pirates," he said. The doc didn't believe him when he said zombies, he thought he was hallucinating from being seasick.

Robert thought to himself, *at least these pirates are defeated, and I can get home through a clear path; If I can find a way, that is.*

Robert had thought he took all the pirates down, destroying the three ships until a receptionist came and said, "There was a pirate attack just hours from the coast, they destroyed an entire ship."

Robert knew he would have to form another crew. He wanted to finish what he started. Since he could take out three of their ships, he knew he would be the right man to finish the job. He would either defeat the pirates and make it home or he would die trying.

Now, he would rest until he got his health back to shape. Then he would form a crew to take to the sea. He didn't have much money, but he would do what he could to get men together, if possible. Until then he would have to rest up because he knew he wasn't in shape to take a second encounter any time soon. He was lucky to make it off the ship as the only known survivor. He wanted to quit when he thought of all his friends being dead, his business gone and family on the other side of the wide ocean blue, and the zombies still haunted the waters. He almost wished he was dead too, but his family gave him the inspiration to make it back along with his passion for storytelling. People would think this one was quite the whopper, but it was true.

WORPHMAN PEN

Worphman Penitentiary was a prison that had stood for over a century. It had seen the likes of some of the worst criminals out there; mad serial killers, dangerous men, and regular men whose crimes were simple petty theft that acted out too much for mainstream. The guards were very tough, but not invincible. Once one guard tried to stop a fight and he was beaten to death. Many prisoners and guards both died in these walls over the years.

Worphmans Pen was in a very desolate mountain range; it went across two giant peaks and was multiple levels. It was made from a mix of block, stone, and concrete. It almost always snowed at the top of the prison. Some prisoners were even held at the top in open cells until they froze to death. That is how they exercised their death penalty. The prisoners and guards came in and out by helicopter. The guards worked two to three weeks at a time, then they got a week off. Some guards even chose to live there. Everyone who resided or worked there was a dead soul; the guards especially, you couldn't have much of a conscious to work at a place like that.

It was said that the rooftop cell was haunted. It was filled with the angry spirits that had died there. It was an awful way to die up there, sitting in the freezing cold in nothing but a short sleeve jumpsuit. The guards gave the prisoners short sleeves and starved them for two days just to make their lives even worse. It was said that even a short time of living in that cell is the worst time you'll ever spend at Worphmans. Not just the frostbite, but for the hauntings they endured.

One night a guard brought a prisoner up to the rooftop cell; dragged him across the floor by his collar. His name was Ben Johnson; he had been framed for murdering his friends at a party. It was a party of rough people and drug dealers. A group of men killed everyone at the house gathering, due to missed drug debts.

Ben got there just after the attack when the cops arrived, they found him on the scene. When they searched him, they discovered he had a submachine gun and a 9mm on him. Since he was there with illegal weapons, had no alibi, and no one was able to ID the criminals, he was sent to one of the worst prisons in the world as an innocent man. During his time at the pen, he got in a fight and punched a man out cold, then he swung at a guard, then Ben Johnson was beaten half to death. That is when they decided to give him the death penalty. They got him back into shape so he could die a healthy man.

One of the guards, Ralph Shroomton dragged Ben across the roof to a cold cell. Ralph and a few other guards kicked him around turning his healthy condition into an awful one. Ralph smacked Ben in the face with his Billy Club and threw him in the hole. While Ben sat in the worst pain he had ever felt, he noticed rotting corpses around him. Then he saw the spirits flying amongst him; they went in and out of his body. He thought it was the sight of death he was seeing, coming through the northern lights. Everything he saw was bright colours of over a hundred men flying around him. It was starting to get to him. He felt like he was going insane; he started to scream, even with no energy. The scream lasted for thirty seconds.

The guards all started laughing, "Just another scum bag dead," they joked with each other.

While he screamed, the spirits of Worphman Pen's death cell started pulling his spirit apart until he finally dropped. After his death, he floated amongst them in the small cell of horrid ghosts. They all flew and screamed, taking up the entire space. The men would be trapped in this cell for eternity. Now, the innocent man Ben Johnson was also stuck in the Hell hole.

After Ben's death, Ralph Shroomton started carrying another man to his awful demise. Yet when Ralph got to the cell and opened the door, the ghost of the innocent Ben Johnson burst through the entire cell freeing the restless spirits of Worphman Pen. They all flew through Ralph and the other guards, dropping them dead where they stood. After that, the ghost spread through the

Prison. Once the ghosts got through the walls, they started opening cell doors. Within seconds, every cell in Worphman Pen was opened. The inmates flooded out in one of the biggest prison riots of all time. Prisoners trampled through the guards.

The guards tried to shoot them, but there were too many to contain. The warden was on his phone from his safe office in the top tower calling for backup. While he was on the phone, a helicopter smashed right threw his office setting flames to the tower.

The riot went on all day until the air support arrived with backup. Once the troops were near the base, they lost control and crashed into the prison. Several helicopters arrived but each of them smashed into the building. After they all crashed, the jail started collapsing into itself on top of all the fighting inmates. While they were rioting, the roof started smashing onto them, until there was nothing but a large pile of rubble in the mountains. After the collapse, all the spirits were set free to roam the mountains.

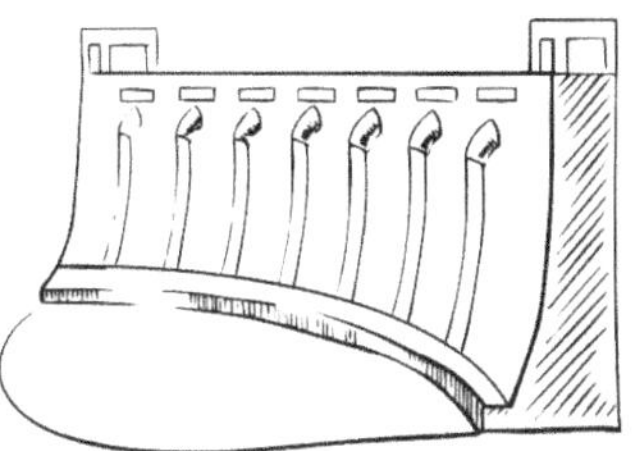

DAM GHOSTS

It was a long hot day in Clarke County, Nevada working on the Boulder Dam. Ryan Freely was a hard-working young man with a sad past. Most of his friends had died on this job. Various accidents had occurred including drowning, explosions going wrong, and some had even died from being hit by a truck and other equipment. Other men simply had heart attacks on the site, due to heat and exhaustion.

One of the bosses was a real jerk. He pushed men way past their limits. He was responsible for several of the deaths that occurred. He was always yelling and cursing, he was making much more money than the average guy, most made less than a dollar an hour. The boss's name was Hugh Bentley; Ryan could not stand the guy. One day, a concrete pour went terribly wrong. Men were slipping with water flying over the edges of the Crawford dam and wooden railings meant to keep men from falling. They didn't have much room for standing demise was inevitable for some.

Hugh Bentley stood back screaming at the men. A few of them were startled by his yelling that they couldn't focus. It was a pour from Hell, maybe one of the worst in history. After the awful work, eleven men fell into the great hole and were submersed into concrete. Hugh did nothing to help or save these men. His anger might have been the reason so many were killed.

Just as they were wrapping up the shift, Ryan started walking away to go home until Hugh started screaming at him to get back to his job. Ryan tried to argue with him, but Hugh kept getting closer and closer walking his big fat body towards him, waving his finger in his face. Ryan kept stepping back until he took one too many steps. Ryan slipped and fell into the wet concrete below. He tried putting his arm out for help, but Hugh just waived his arm in the air, hrugged, and walked away.

Hugh left the site, stopped off for a bite to eat at a nearby bar, then headed for his home in his fancy car. When he stepped through his front door a gust of wind came in smashing every window in his house. It knocked him to the ground, and he felt an awful cold chill. His wife let out a horrible scream and came running down the stairs asking him what had happened.

He told her, "The wind must have picked up."

"That's one angry wind," she said. "And cold."

"Ahhh, clean this crap up! And plastic wrap it 'till we get new windows. I'm going to bed." He didn't spend much time with his wife and headed off to bed.

The next morning, he woke up and got ready for work as usual. He jumped in his fancy automobile and drove off to the dam. He started yelling at people for being late, others for taking time off, and for some, he just liked yelling at them. The whole day he was crusty as could be. Another cement pour was taking place and he was out screaming and yelling. It was almost like he was trying to make people fall in, but this time, the pour went much more successfully. Nobody fell in, that is until Hugh grabbed onto a young man and screamed in his face. He yelled and yelled until a large force of wind separated the two. It knocked Hugh right over the edge. Hugh fell down hundreds of feet into the Colorado River. The kid landed on safe ground. A foreman ran over and picked him up on his shoulder. Then the foreman cheered.

"Let's give it up for this guy, he finally got rid of Hugh Bentley. Then everyone cheered as he put the kid back on the ground. After the cheering calmed down the foreman then said, "And get this guy a beer right now, we need a break to celebrate. That mean, old S.O.B finally got what was coming to him!" The foreman looked around and saw the workers start to relax. He piped up and shouted, "Hey you guys, get back to work, this guy gets a break, not you guys."

TIKAANI

In the Inuit village of Tikaani, they considered the wolf their sacred beast. Before this, the wolf had run wild for many years destroying the people of Tikaani. Until one day, a man named Amaruq befriended the wolves; he eventually lived with them and grew a connection with all wolves. He became their leader he was able to keep them tame and not attack the people of his tribe. The wolves never bothered the Tikaani people after that. He had saved his people's lives from the wolves.

One day, he was running with the wolves when a family was being attacked by a polar bear. A man was stricken down and the wife and two kids were about to be next until Amaruq sent the pack of wolves on the bear. While one wolf is no match for a polar bear, twenty wolves can easily take a polar bear down. They ripped him apart before he could attack the family anymore. The man survived the attack but as he went to his savior, Amaruq was gone in a flash.

He had saved people on other occasions as well. When he would see someone falling, drowning, or being attacked, he would command his family of wolves to help. He protected the land with his wolf family until he eventually grew old and died. He never left the pack though.

Years after his death people started to finally realize Amaruq was dead as nobody ever saw him anymore. People still reported seeing tame wolves walk right past them without even a growl. Still, on occasion, a wolf would save someone's life if they encountered a bear or other predators. A wolf even came up to a man once at camp and started eating the meat he was cooking beside him. The camper gave him another piece of meat right out of his hand. Things like this happened all the time around there. For generations, the wolves lived at peace with the people of Tikaani. A legend started that the ghost of

Amaruq kept the wolves and humans at peace. His spirit kept the wolves calm for centuries. It was forbidden to kill a wolf anywhere in the region of Tikaani, because it became their sacred beast. People often spoke about the legend. Children were told this story and it was enforced on them to never kill a wolf.

But one day, a young man named Qimmiq, still under the age of eighteen, grew tired of hearing these legends. He liked to kill whatever he could get his hands on. He was a great hunter. He even had polar bear furs in his collection after he had killed a few with his spear. He was a natural hunter and liked to kill for fun. It was just a part of him. He went out for rabbits often, mainly for target practice, yet he provided for the people of his home with musk ox, walrus, and bears. Now, he wanted to kill a wolf to add to his list.

No one would ever help him when he said he wanted to kill a wolf; no one would let him, it was taboo. One night he decided he needed a wolf skin. He went out looking on his own. It was snowing so he travelled deep into the snowstorm. He brought three spears with him, two of them were for throwing the other he would keep near for close combat. He followed the tracks in the snow, and he found a pack of five wolves. He planned to throw a spear at one of the wolves.

At first, the wolves started making their way to him in a friendly manner. They were going to befriend him. But Qimmiq had no intentions of befriending them. He threw a spear at the closest one, it went right through its heart dropping him. He was so proud of himself; the first man to kill a wolf in generations.

He was filled with joy until the dark sky closed in on him. A huge gust of purple wind surrounded him. A large face of a wolf appeared in front of him. It howled in his face while wolves gathered around him. The howl brought him to his knees, it was the sound that nightmares were made of. It screeched in his ears for what seemed to feel like an hour for him; the torture was extreme until his brain finally gave out on him.

Then a howl let loose across the entire village. The people were shocked by the noise as the town started filling with snow. Wolves began appearing all over. They came out of the mountains. Hundreds of them appeared, surrounding the entire village. The howls let loose all over the region of Tikaani. As the first, set of wolves moved closer, and hundreds more kept appearing. Soon the wolves moved in close to the village. The people moved into their huts to hide. But when the first wolf attacked, it broke through a hut. Then the beast started ripping a man apart. It would then go on to do the same thing to his whole family. More wolves started doing this across the Tikaani village. A few men grabbed spears knowing they had to break the sacred rule. But as soon as a man stabbed a wolf in the chest, darkness encompassed the town followed by a flash of lightning.

Each wolf made its mark; hundreds of wolves came in and overran everyone quickly. The two hundred men and women of Tikaani were all eaten alive due to one man's foolishness and arrogance. After the town was slaughtered, a great light flashed over it, submersing the entire village. It blew apart every building in Tikaani.

After the destruction, there were two hundred wolf pups running around the free land of Tikaani.

Red Bird Woods

Larry and Scott Daniels ran a forestry company that mainly entailed commercial lot clearing jobs. The Daniel's tree service had destroyed many forests in its fifteen years of business. The brothers travelled across the country with their crew putting bids on jobs. One day, a job came up that nobody wanted to touch; Scott got the call.

The potential client told him he had just bought a few thousand acres of land to build a development, and a highway extending from the city to the project. This land was once home to a large tribe of indigenous people. Now, it was just a very large forest known as the Red Bird Woods. It was surrounded by a field on one side and the Rocky Mountains on the other side. This forest was in Alberta, a province in Canada. The Daniels' company was stationed in Ontario, a couple of provinces away. It was necessary that the client select a company from so far away, as anyone nearby knew of the legends of the Red Bird Forest. The stories were that anyone who had entered the forest in the last century never came out.

The Daniels brothers had never heard of the legend, so they agreed to do a video consultation for a quote. The client showed them video footage of the Red Bird Woods. The two brothers decided to take the job and put in a very high bid. The client didn't take it right away because he didn't want to look too desperate. So, he waited until the next day to reach out and confirm the job.

Scott and Larry called their crew together and readied them to haul across the country. Later that week, they were packed and ready to go. They had six trucks, three standard chippers, a tub chipper, two skid steers, and a log truck with attachments for removing stumps and picking up wood.

A young native man on the crew called Scott the night before they left. He told him he could not attend because he had just found stories of the Red Bird Woods and warned him not to go. Scott said that was okay if he didn't want to go, but it wasn't stopping the rest of the team.

The Daniels brothers hauled ass across Canada for three days until they arrived at the Red Bird Woods. When they got there, they had to drive very far into the wilderness from where they were staying, and that only got them to the entrance of the forest, there was still more distance to cover; it was a great-sized wooded area. Scott and Larry decided they would have to set up camp there. Scott was a lazy worker, he hauled back to town in the pickup truck.

He made any excuse he could find to get away and avoid physical labour.

Scott drove into town; it took him until noon to get there. When he got there, he started talking to a native man. Scott told him what he needed for supplies and where he was working.

The man told him, "You need to get your men out of there now. No one comes out of that forest alive."

Scott just agreed with the man who was insisting that he get out of there. As Scott started leaving, he thought that is the second person to mention the curse. He told himself, I'll let my brother know these stories when I get back to him.

While Scott went into town, Larry got his men started on felling trees. They flopped them all day having a great time. One of the workers noticed an ancient arrowhead and some large rocks with tribal markings on them. He called everyone over to come to take a look. Larry and a few other guys came over. When the man went to pick it up, the air around the workers plummeted to below freezing. Then shocking light flashed across the forest putting everyone in a daze. Larry was completely frightened; he did not want to be working there.

When Scott got back to the site, he saw Larry and the boys were starting to pack it up. Scott went over and let him know the stories he had heard.

He said to him, "I heard some rumours that this place is haunted."

Larry responded, "Yeah, I think the rumours are true, we just saw a flash of light. We're getting out of here."

"Sounds like a good idea."

The two of them used their phone with a satellite booster and were soon on a video chat with the client. They told him they were getting out of there because it was haunted.

He replied to them by saying, "That rumour is a bunch of crap. If you leave, you will be getting millions of dollars' worth of fines."

The boys gulped and told him they would get back to work. When the brothers told the crew they were staying, they were not happy at all. Scott told them they could walk home if they wanted, but they weren't borrowing a truck. The workers stayed, but they were miserable to the two brothers all night. Some stayed mad the whole time.

The crew just bore through it. Scott and Larry were just as mad as the rest of them, but they really didn't want to get those fines, which they knew could happen.

So, they kept working; three days in, nothing went wrong. They cleared a good chunk out in those few days. They found more artifacts, but they were not allowed to touch anything that looked sacred. Everyone listened to this advice.

On their fourth day in, they got to a large opening in the wood. Here there were great-sized redwoods. There were carvings of faces on many of the trees.

They looked ancient.

A man yelled," We can't cut those things down."

Scott yelled back, "We got no choice here."

"Well, I'm not doing it. I'm getting the hell out of here," the man responded.

"Fine, get the hell out of here. I'll cut it down."

The man started walking back to the camp while Scott started up his chain saw. He had a really bad feeling about this. He revved it up and approached the first tree. He dug his 66 into the tree to start the notch. Purple chips started spitting out of the back of the saw and flew into the sky. Then the chainsaw busted into flames setting Scott on fire.

He screamed for his life while burning to death. The men started running, but the purple chips kept blowing into a fine dust that submersed them completely. The men coughed and yelled. The spirits came awake and haunted them, purple air filling the entire forest. Men at the camp saw it closing in on them. They started to run but the ghostly smog struck them down to the ground. Then the spirits of the Red Bird Woods tortured them all as well. Trees started growing tall from the old tree stumps.

Every worker at the site started feeling tremendous pain. Roots from the ground came up and started pulling men apart until they submersed into the earth of the forest.

The workers of Daniels Tree Company had all become sunken into the soil and a part of the natural earth. The Red Bird Forest grew thicker than ever with every tree back in position. Saplings even started growing where the men had fallen.

Later, when the client tried to get a hold of them no one answered. No matter how much he tried, he never could. He tried to get another contractor, but it took him months to get someone ignorant enough to go. When he spoke with the other tree company, the contractor told him he only does his quotes in person with the customer, at the site.

ST. JOSEPH'S CATHEDRAL

For forty years Father Woodley worked at St. Joseph's cathedral. For the past twenty, he was the only priest to reside there on his own. Sometimes, other priests would come down and help in a mass, but he was the only priest employed directly by the church who also lived on the premise.

During the first half of his time at St. Joseph's, he served under Father Patty. One night, Father Patty died in the church without warning. The next Sunday, the parishioners wondered where Father Patrick was. Father Woodley went to his room and saw Father Patty lying lifeless in his bed. Father Woodley went back down to give the sermon but

Father Woodley finished his sermon by saying, "May the spirit of Father Patty flow through this church always."

Father Woodley was soon after appointed as the leading priest of St. Joseph's cathedral. He was asked if he would like another to take over or if he wanted a young priest to help him with his duties. He denied both requests and then became the only priest in his church. It was up to him to lead his flock.

One night, shortly after Father Patty's death, Father Woodley was sitting in his bed thinking about how the spirits flow through the church. He thought about how he and the other priests spoke of spirits and just thought of it as part of the bible; he didn't actually think the place to be filled with ghosts. He thought of it as the divine holy spirit that flowed through the great beautiful church of God. He believed true congregates would always be a part of this holy building. Father Patty had told him that he had seen the ghosts flow through the church; that they spoke to him, and he talked back to them. Again, Woodley just thought of this as the Word of God, from the Good Book.

That night while sitting up in his dormitory trying to get some rest, Father Patty appeared.

He said, "Son, now you are the leader of this flock and the keeper of the beauty in this house of God. You will start to know the spirits of the cathedral." A chubby man named Bob popped out of the wall with a friendly "hello" and then introduced himself. Next, a woman named Sylvia came out of the same wall and did the same.

Last, a little person came out of the ground and let out a bursting, "How ya doin'? I'm little Will."

Father Patty spoke again and said, "Now you know the words I spoke to be true, always believe in what you preach as seeing is believing. Now enjoy the rest of your evening, we will be seeing you in this house of God."

There were a dozen ghosts that lived in the house of God. Bob, Sylvia, and Will were his closest friends. The others came around sometimes, but those three were always with him. Father Patty did not come around too often, only on holidays and funerals But although those were the only times he made his presence known; Father Woodley always sensed he was around.

One day, an awful gangster by the name of Vinnie suffered an awful stabbing, after murdering two people. He died in an awful fit of rage. He was to be buried at the cemetery. He had awful ways about him, there were rumours he worshiped the devil. Vinnie's parents were good, kind people and generous to the church. The parents insisted that their son would be buried there and the ceremony to be held at the church. Father Woodley could not turn them down; it was not the way of the church to do such a thing.

Just before the service, Father Patty showed himself to Father Woodley. Father Patty told him not to give this man a blessing.

Father Woodley thought I could not do such an awful thing. Father Patty disappeared immediately after giving this message.

When the service was underway, many crooked people were there amongst the parents and their few friends. The people were covered in dark, satanic tattoos. Father Woodley could see dark clouds following each of these lost souls. Vinnie was carried down the aisle by his father at the front, two uncles behind, and on the other sides, there were three scary-looking specimens of men, one with a mohawk, one bald, and another with a mop of hair so long you couldn't even see his face. Father Woodley was terrified just watching them walk up to place the casket in front of the mourners.

As the pallbearers got closer, Father Woodley noticed the pentagrams on their foreheads.

He thought, how in God's name could I let these people into my beautiful home, the house of God? When he started the sermon, he did the normal rituals, but he just didn't feel right while speaking to this crowd. He saw Vinnie's mother weeping, and he believed that she deserved to hear the words he had to say. But inside, just from looking at Vinnie, Father Woodley knew every positive word about this man was a lie. When it came time to close the casket, Father Woodley decided he would give him God's blessing.

Before he did this, Father Patty appeared again and said, "I tell you this one more time my child. Do not bless this man. Father Woodley ignored him. Woodley went on to bless him. But when he touched his forehead, he noticed the number of the beast, across the skin of his skull tucked under his hair. The corpse started shaking as he did this.

Then he thought to himself again, I know I shouldn't, but I bless everyone in my church. After he blessed him just over the number, something awful happened, a shining light blasted out of the casket. Father Woodley let out an awful scream. All the friends of Vinnie started to grow demonic tails and their faces became even more hideous. Dark light shined from all their bodies, and the church went dark.

These worshipers were no longer human, they were demons of the beast. They started walking through the church, then started to grab onto the innocent members biting them. As a result, they started to become demons as well. Evil ghouls started appearing in the air. The ghosts of the church came and tried to intervene, but the dark ghouls overpowered them. Soon Father Woodley was surrounded by ghouls in the air, and the demons would be on top of him. He hated himself in these moments for turning his church into a building of hell, but he only did what he thought was right in his heart.

He thought he would soon turn into a demon until he saw five angels. The angels started shaking a chandelier until it came loose. As it fell, four statues, Jesus, Mother Marry, and two angels all came down as well and smashed into the pews of the church. It smashed over half of the attendants. Still, demons walked towards Father Woodley until an incredible burst of lightning flashed across the room.

Father Woodley saw every devilish being get sucked into the chandelier and statues. The light temporarily blinded Father Woodley. Once the light was gone, Father Woodley noticed that the church was back to normal, and Vinnie's family sat in the pews watching as the only audience. They had no clue of what just had happened, and Father Woodley sensed that. So, he started again from where he felt was right. The body of Vinnie was no longer in the casket, it had vanquished along with the demons, but no one needed to know that.

At the end of the funeral in the cemetery, Vinnie's mother, father, and little sister came up to him, to thank him for hosting the funeral. Vinnie's sister was just young. While she cried, she thanked Father Woodley for hosting them. Father Woodley walked away and left them to grieve in the graveyard. In the distance, Father Woodley looked back and saw Vinnie's sister looking at him. When he caught eyes with the little girl, the face of the beast flashed before him.

After Woodley realized the girl was possessed, Father Patty appeared. Father Patty told him, "You should have listened to me in the first place."

He then disappeared.

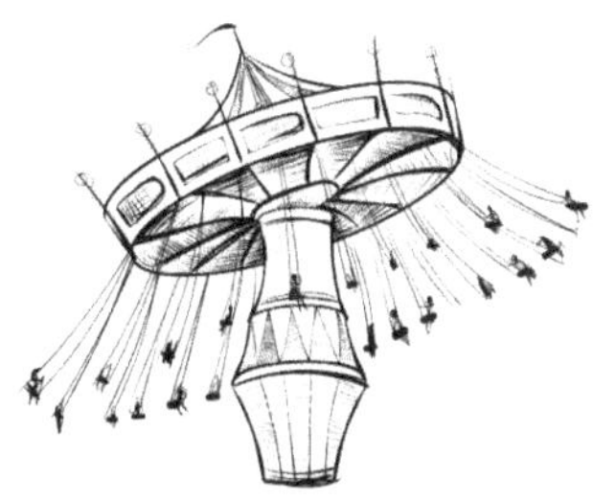

Kai Park

The name's Andy. I did construction for a while before I switched to janitorial duty at The Sports World Arena and Aquatics Centre, in a little town called Hopkinsville. In Hopkinsville, there was a large park called Kai Park. It was on the side of the busiest street in town, Parkton Road. The park was named after a millionaire, Ronny Kai. He had lived in Hopkinsville in the 1920s and willed his money and land to the town with a clause that it would always be an exhibition ground. The city used to have an annual exhibition every summer, including farming events. There was a beautiful grandstand it filled every year with the Hopkinsville

Rodeo; the town had a large farming community and was very community-friendly. It was a good friend of mine who told me the story of Kai Park and its name.

I should have taken more consideration when I was offered a position in building the Sports World Arena. The new mayor of Hopkinsville came in with many promises. She told the town she would get rid of crime and drug addiction, she had a plan, she said.

That plan included bringing a bunch of homeless to the town from the largest city in the country. The city's mayor offered Miss Yates of Hopkinsville a large amount of money to do this; other cities got involved as well. She moved bums in from all over by bus and placed them in front of the YMCA in the heart of downtown. She gave them all tents and blankets and let them take right over.

That was just one of her asinine ideas; I could tell you many. Her biggest mistake was selling the rights of the arena title to a large franchise like Sports World, instead of keeping it an exhibition ground like the original owner Ronnie Kai wanted. She couldn't even name it after him.

When she made the announcement that she would be building a new recreational centre on the Ronnie

Kai' exhibition ground. I always wondered if a recreational building was the same as an exhibition ground. I guess the city thought they were close enough. I got a call from the construction union to work on this job. I thought it was a good idea because it was close to home. When I started, a lot of people were not happy about her selling the name to Sports World. A lot of people were upset, but not for the right reason. The townspeople were mainly mad because they didn't want to see a stupid sign on their local arena. Very few actually knew the history of the park.

While I worked there, there were two fatalities on different occasions. One time, a crane dropped a load right on top of a guy in a freak accident, and the cable just snapped. The other time, a man was killed by a large concrete form falling out of place and landing on top of him. It was another freak accident. Every time those accidents happened, the equipment was all inspected and the forms had been installed properly.

I thought about quitting, but I didn't. A few other guys did, they were smart. The mayor came out and told us we would get an extra five dollars an hour to stay on. I thought it was a no-brainer to take it. I guess it was a no-brain decision because, in hindsight, I can see I wasn't using my brain. The job went awfully rough for just a rec centre. Bricks would fly off scaffolding with large gusts of wind. One man even got blown off some scaffolding on a beautiful day and he broke his shoulder. He sued the city. I guess the mayor's rec centre was worth all the havoc to her, just like the homeless problem.

Once the job was finally done, I was so relieved. Then a city representative offered me a job at the arena. They offered it to me because I was one of the only workers that stayed the whole way through the construction job, and of course, I was the only one willing to take the job. They offered me a great position, and better pay, and it was much easier than construction. They told me all I would be doing is cleaning the place, doing some gardening, and doing a bit of maintenance on the pool. Again, this was a no-brainer for me.

The week before the grand opening, I was in there quite a lot. I made sure the pool was nice and clean, the ice was nice and fresh, and the temperature was good to go. It was a shame to see such nice ice suffer as the owner increased the temperature to suit the audience's needs. My good friend told me that in his day, the city arena was open air. That's right, it was an old barn-style building. They would keep the windows open at night after giving it a good flood. He told me it was always freezing cold, you had to layer up. But that didn't stop the people of Hopkinsville from gathering every week to see the local minor A team play.

I was speaking to a man outside the arena one day; we stopped and had a cigarette together. I was smoking a colt, I was never one for cigarettes, only if I was stressed and there were no colts around. The man asked me if I had ever heard of Ronnie Kai. I told him I had heard of him.

He replied to me by saying, "You be careful. I don't think Ronnie Kai would like the name of his park being changed to an overpriced, overrated conglomerate."

You know, as he said that I got a great chill down my spine. When I started walking back to the arena, a huge gust of wind came flying at me and it had an even worse chill to it. I went inside and the lights flickered.

I thought it was strange for a new building to have failing lights already. Maybe the electricians were too burnt out to know what they were doing.

Some more weird things started happening while I was on the first week of maintenance. Water started splashing from the pool, the pump failed a few times. Then I just started thinking, the mayor must have really cheaped out.

On the night of the first hockey game and opening ceremony of the Sports World Arena and Aquatics, that stood on the former Kai Park, the mayor was giving a speech. As she spoke, the buzzer started going off. People started booing her for the crappy arena. Once she started walking away while being booed, she tripped and fell, or maybe she was pushed over. Anyway, everyone laughed, including me. She left unhappy after the anthem was sung. Next, the lights went out. Everyone was startled, but I wasn't too worried. I just thought she was being cheap until there was a large smash and the light flashed back on. Everyone screamed. The large score box had come down and flattened the anthem singer. The fire alarm rang, and the arena needed to be evacuated.

A few days later, I was at the arena, cleaning the pool. I was coming in from a smoke when I heard an awful scream from the ice rink. I ran over to see what was going on. I came up to the glass where the door to the ice was. I saw the mayor being run over by Zamboni along with a city inspector. There was no one on the ice machine. It was then that I realized that Ronnie Kai was not happy with the Sports World Arena and Aquatic Centre.

I realized too late to do anything about what was happening. The air went colder than any arena I had ever felt before; the wind swirled through the place. The door I was leaning against flew open, and I slipped onto the ice. Then I started getting pushed closer to the Zamboni. Soon it picked up its speed and ran me over to my awful demise.

I now permanently reside at the Sports World Arena and Aquatics. I have grown to become great friends with Ronnie Kai. He reminded me of another friend I once had. I keep him pretty calm these days. The only haunting we do now is to throw popcorn at people, sometimes blowing up the machine and making the popcorn fly all over. We also like knocking over people's drinks and spraying water at people in the washrooms. We laugh quite a bit. Ronnie Kai learned from me that there are other ways to haunt and still have fun.

THE SCARECROW'S NEIGHBOUR

It stood up from the ground on a post with its two arms spread. It didn't look friendly; it looked miserable. Of course, it did. There were a dozen crows spread across it, even one on its rotting pumpkin-for-a-head. The pumpkin had an awful grin. It seemed to always stare at me. I couldn't help but stare back.

Every day I sat in my office. It was on the second floor of my home. It was an old brick farmhouse with two floors, except there was no farm. I sold off all the farmland to the neighbour when I moved here. That kind of life is too much work for me. I kept a few acres of land and enjoy my large country home with my few gardens. But if there is one thing I hate, it's that God-awful scarecrow.

Right next door, on the side of my fence, the neighbour has it sitting just near the property line. It faces right towards me. Sometimes, I wonder if he put it there just to freak me out. Some of these farmers had a weird sense of humour. But then I thought, maybe it had more than a joke for me, maybe it had a story to tell. I kept thinking about that while I did my work. But as I kept thinking, it started to get to me.

I was walking down my backyard one day grabbing some clothes off the line. I wasn't married, so I did these kinds of chores on my own. The ugly scarecrow stared right at me with its ripped blue plaid jacket blowing stuffing out to the wind. When I turned my back to the figure, I saw a very dark tall shadow towering over me. I turned to look, and the scarecrow was standing five feet above me. I let out a gasp, then I heard a laugh. I looked down and Leroy the farmer was underneath adjusting it.

He said to me, "Stanley I didn't know how easily you startled." I kind of chuckled, then walked away without a response.

The next day, I knew he was trying to mess with me. I went outside to have a coffee, and a smoke on the back porch.

The second I sat and got comfortable, I saw the jerk put up seven more scarecrows on the property line, facing right at me. I should have never given him the satisfaction when he startled me the first time.

Farmer Leroy once had two sons and a wife. Now, he was a widower, and his two sons had died in separate wars. He was just a lonely old man now. I guess the only friends he had were the scarecrows. And getting a laugh out of me was his only enjoyment. Sometimes, I wish I never sold him the land. He likes blowing leaves and snow on my lawn.

He also throws his old chewed-up tobacco over the fence. He would always laugh at me when I did something foolish, and then he would give me a thumbs up.

The next night, the autumn wind was strong. I sat down in my bed and looked out my window. I noticed all eight of the scarecrows blowing in the wind, watching me; they really gave me the creeps. I read a bit of my book, enjoying the cold wind blowing in through my window. When I put the book down and went to close the window for the night, I only counted five scarecrows. Now, I really had the chills, and I was starting to fill with fright.

I just thought to myself, I guess I have been working too much. I can't even keep count of things anymore. Just before I fell asleep, I saw a great flash of blue light. I just thought it was my dreams starting for the night.

While I slept, three of the scarecrows came to life. The three ghosts of Leroy's family took the form of burlap creatures. His two sons and his wife visited him. At first, they spoke to Leroy, having a great conversation, but then they told him he should join them. His life was so boring they decided it would be better for him. Leroy's scarecrow family grabbed onto him. He let out an awful scream while he made his transformation.

His awful screams woke me up. I looked out the window and saw bolts of lightning through the calm night. Then the other remaining scarecrows came to life and started walking towards my home. I grabbed my shotgun and pointed it out the window. I started firing at the monsters. I kept shooting, but they kept moving closer. The only effect it had was some of the stuffing came loose.

I hoped, maybe enough stuffing might fly out. Then as I was shooting at them, one approached my porch. I grabbed the machete I had stored in my nightstand; reloaded the gun and headed downstairs to face them head-on. I ran out of my bedroom and right in front of me appeared farmer Leroy. He stood in front of me covered in burlap, his head full of worms crawling through it. I took my machete and stabbed him in the stomach, more worms came out. Then, I was surrounded by his family of three scarecrows, they grabbed me by the throat, my two sides, and my back. I let out a horrid cry as I fell to the ground with my body turning to burlap. All eight scarecrows stood on top of me, ripping at my skin, as each peel turned into fabric. The last memory I had was standing on a post with the other eight scarecrows.

A shiver went up my spine, what an awful thought. I looked out the window one more time at the scarecrow standing on its lonesome.

I hit save on my laptop and thought to myself, thank God ghosts aren't real. I grabbed my lighter and pack of smokes, and then I headed to the porch. But as I walked out my bedroom door, that's when they got me.

SUPERNATURAL DISASTER

I moved forward. There was nothing but purple haze around me. As I looked through the woods, the haze just grew thicker. I could see trees and wildlife, but it was being masked by darkness.

I was stranded in the woods; I stood in a nightmare thinking, *where am I, how did I get here, what is this place?* I even thought, *who am I?*

I felt like my mind had left my body. Everything was a haze of different colours now. I walked through the woods following the shadows that lurked. I was terrified, but my curiosity drew me closer. When I reached the moving shadow, I became surrounded by ghouls.

They lurked around me, laughing, then they spun and threw my mind like a swarm of bees in the brain. Before I knew it, my human spirit was destroyed. Now I was a ghoul, a demon, a monster of a beast.

There was a large demon that led the way. He was the face of a dark red and black skull, with bright yellow fire blazing from his eyes. In a way, it looked as if the beast Satan had appointed this ghoul himself. I realized that I was a haunter; that was what my afterlife was bound for, haunting the earth with a pack of demons.

We raised hell every night. The first night of my haunting ways, we lurked in the woods where I was first acquainted with the ghouls. We glided through the trees, darkening everything in our path. We spooked the deer that lived in the woods, and those that died joined our army of demons. Soon we possessed all the wildlife in the forest. Now we had to take over the people of the woods, for our ultimate plan.

First, we saw some campers. We latched ourselves onto them and made them our slaves. They became the walking living dead. After they suffered, they were ours. We did the same to a few camps of lumberjacks, as well as some cottagers staying at their cabins.

Then we went to haunt a house. A family sat there by the fireplace telling stories. A half a dozen of us swirled around them, they trembled in complete fear. The mother held her children as they cowered in terror. The father went to grab his shotgun off the mantle. I jumped on top of him and let out an awful ghostly howl, and then I sucked the life out of him. He lay on the ground, nothing more than a zombie. He was a part of our divine plan now. We would take the town with our new demonic minions, along with the demonic deer and bears of the woods.

After the entire forest was taken over and infected by our plague, we marched to the village. We stood out front with the small army that had been formed. Our leader, the miniature devil, screamed. Then he blasted towards the town. The deer stampeded through the village, destroying anyone in their path. Then they rammed through the buildings while the bears attacked the houses and people inside. We, the demons, set fire to the buildings and spread it across the town. We gusted over the structures after setting the flames. Everyone in the town that was now dead, dying, or in severe pain. As they suffered, we tortured them one last time while they turned into the minions we all were.

As the screams ended, the clouds remained dark with tremendous thunder. Lighting started blasting into flames. The storm grew quicker by the second; we started spinning through the town; all of us turned into one. An incredible cyclone storm barged through the remainder of the village. All of us were the cyclone. The twister spun right through the crust of the ground and into the deep lava that lies below.

The next day a media storm hit the destroyed town and said it was the biggest tornado to ever hit the area. Of course, I know it was no ordinary tornado. But maybe every storm and disaster aren't natural, maybe they are all supernatural.

THE DOLLS OF THE COAST

---

ay over in the Atlantic Maritimes, there were three lobstermen out in the Great Atlantic. Randy, and his two sons Gary and Paul, spend their days unloading traps. Gary was twenty years old, and Paul was seventeen. When they finished for the day and arrived home, they had a huge loot of delicious lobsters.

The family had a large beachfront property. There was a large dock off to the side of the beach where they kept the boats and unloaded the cargo. They let part of their beach be used by the public. Here, they had a gift shop and snack bar where they sold lobster wraps and sandwiches. In the gift shop, they sold a variety of shells and collectibles from the sea, along with coconut dolls, sea paintings, and other interesting knick-knacks. There was a large house on the property where Randy and his wife, Linda, lived. Paul and Gary each had a small shack set up that they lived in on their own.

When the three men arrived back at the dock, they noticed Linda over at the beach, she was gathered with a few friends that were visiting. The men noticed that it looked like she was inspecting something. There were a bunch of mysterious items scattered across the beach. The three fishermen couldn't make it out at first, but when they got off the boat, Linda started waving a doll at them. From where they were standing, it looked like there was a black shadow casting over her and the doll in her hand. For a moment, she looked like an awful witch carrying the thing, but it was just a quick glance. She had an ecstatic look on her face while waving the doll. The men each felt like the doll gave them the creeps and they kind of shrugged at each other. The boys always thought their mom was a little nuts with the knick-knacks. She spent most of her time making and collecting things for her craft shack. As Randy, Paul, and Gary walked to the end of the dock, Linda ran over to them with the doll in her hand.

She said, "Hey guys, look what washed up on shore." She pointed over to the beach, where there were a hundred dolls laid along the shore. She told them that while she was in the shack, she had heard an awful gust of wind that shook the small building. She said when she walked out, she saw a few waves. At first, she thought it was kelp. After the waves ceased, she walked over and noticed what she described as beautiful, antique dolls.

Linda told them how happy she was with her find. The men of the family knew exactly what she would do with them, put them in her shop.

Randy and his sons unloaded the boat and cleaned up the rest of the day, while Linda cleaned up the dolls. They were ugly and creepy, they had dark ratty clothes covered in kelp. After she got them cleaned up, she stripped the ragged clothes off them. Then she put her own outfits on them. She had made up sailor and fishermen raincoats, and other east coast outfits. She had had them made for a while, now she finally got to use them.

Linda spent the whole night cleaning the dolls, and while she didn't get them all finished, she was able to start putting some on the shelves of her shop.

The next morning in the shop, an ugly, wretched-looking woman came into the shop while the men were at sea. She grabbed one of the dolls and started waving it around.

The woman screamed, "These are my dolls!!!"

Linda walked over to her and asked if she needed a hand with something. The woman went to push Linda, then screamed again. "These are mine! Give them back! Aaaaggghh!!!"

Linda replied, "Excuse me miss, but you know the law of the sea, finders keepers. Now, could you please leave my store, unless you want to buy them back?"

"To hell with you! You have no right to these; they were taken from me by the living winds. They're alive and they'll get you." She screeched.

Then the wretched woman screamed a loud gasp and turned into a bright but dark flash before she disappeared. Linda screamed she couldn't believe what she had seen, and she knew no one else would believe it for she was the only one in the shop that day. Most days she worked on her own. And since the wicked woman was the first customer of the day, there were no witnesses to what she had seen.

Randy and the boys didn't come back until late

afternoon, before supper. Linda kept what she had seen to herself, until that night when she and Randy were lying in bed. She told him how the wicked woman came in and screamed and flashed away like a ghost. When she told him this, he just stared blankly at her. He didn't want to believe her. He thought she was nuts, but there was part of him that knew it to be true. When he had seen those ugly dolls, he immediately had a terrible feeling.

He told her not to think about it, "Maybe you're seasick," he told her with a chuckle.

She punched him in the arm and said, "Whatever." Then she curled up away from him, tucked her head into the pillow, and pretended to sleep. She tried her best to rest, but all she could think about was the woman and the dolls. She was even starting to wonder if she herself was nuts.

All night, she lay there with visions of the dolls crawling on top of her and filling her home. She thought she was asleep dreaming until she realized she was just lying with her eyes closed letting her imagination run wild.

That's when the window flew open. She jumped up to see what it was. She tried waking up Randy, but he shrugged her away; he was exhausted from all his time on the salt water. Linda returned to the window and looked again. She didn't see anything; the wind was calm. She was bewildered by the situation She stared out of the window for a minute, shaking her head at the mystery. Then the face of the wretched woman appeared, laughing at her. Shortly after, she heard screams and shots being fired. It sounded like her sons were in trouble. She went to grab her gun from the closet when three dolls jumped on her face, scratching, and viciously attacking her. She tried pulling them off, but they took her to the ground and tormented her. The screams she let out awoke her husband. He jumped out of bed and ran over. He went to kick one and it grabbed onto his leg biting at it. The gunshots and screams from outside stopped.

A huge gust of wind blew into the room. It knocked Randy over to the wall followed by ninety-seven dolls that flew through the window and landed on both Randy and his wife, Linda. He tried fighting back against them, but they ripped him into little shreds. The remains were so small that the dolls carried the pieces of bodies with them back to the ocean. All the dolls, along with the family, were taken back into the ocean blue to rest, for God knows how long.

The next day, one of Linda's employees came to help in the gift shack. The employee noticed the shop wasn't open yet, and Randy's boat was still docked. It was very strange for the family to not be working. The worker knocked on the door, but there was no answer. She waited there all day; she tried calling every phone they had. After hours of no answer, the employee called the police. The authorities waited two days to file a missing person's report. When there was still no sign of them, the cops came and investigated their disappearance. The detectives searched the entire property, but all they found was a doll sitting under the dock. It wore a diamond engagement ring on three of its fingers. The cops declared a regional search to be conducted across the entire maritime region and put out an international missing person's report. It was the strangest disappearance the officers had ever seen.

One of the officers took the doll that was found under the doc back to his children. Eventually, he and his family went missing as well. Now it really might be the strangest mystery to ever hit the East Coast.

THE CREMATORIUM

The fire rose greatly; the heat was unbearable for anyone. First, the body melted before it crisped and turned to ash. After the fire did its job, a bell rang. The cremator pulled out the ashes of a deceased man. He put them into a basket to be packaged, sealed and jarred. The cremator was twenty-seven years old. He had been burning bodies for the last ten years since he was seventeen.

Dylan had tried working other jobs before he started doing this, but he couldn't seem to find the right fit. He would either get fired or get in a fight. When he started at the crematorium, he was nervous; he was worried about messing with dead bodies. Dylan had always wondered about spirits, ghosts, and hauntings. He was never a firm believer in anything, but he believed enough to be worried about a crematorium.

The day he started he was mortified at the first sight of a dead body. He had a hard time getting over the smell. After a week of learning how to prepare the dead and run the furnace, he got over his fears and started to get the hang of things.

Throughout his ten years of working there, his suspicion of spirits became firmer. Weird things would happen. First, the oven gave out much more often than it should. Remains would scatter across the floor sometimes. But the weirdest thing he experienced was the chill he would feel every time he touched a body. Even though the oven was boiling the room, he could feel death's cold touch every time he sent someone to become charcoal. There was one time he was sending the body of an old woman into the hot incinerator; he swore he felt the grasp of her arm latch onto him. Then an awful frightening look flashed across her face. It only lasted for a second; he thought he was going nuts. He figured he would just pretend all these scenarios were figments of his imagination.

Yet one day, he once again changed his mind. There was no doubt that he was now a believer in spirits and ghosts. After ten years of working there, he had seen something that turned him paler than a ghost itself. He was throwing a body in the oven for its final rest when it latched onto him. The cold body grabbed his throat, pulled Dylan down to its mouth, and breathed cold air in his ear.

The talking corpse whispered to him in a frightful tone while still holding tightly to his throat, "This was not my wish, my family cheaped out."

Dylan pushed himself off the body with all his might. After he escaped from the corpse's grasp, he whipped the body and the tray into the oven. But before he could shut the door, he fell backwards to the ground. He lay on his back for a moment in shock, then he slowly got up and saw the body burst into flames. With the oven door open, he could see the fire blazing. The face of a demon came popping out, and with an awful scream, the flames and the face blinded him while smoke filled the room making him cough and gasp for air. The demon tortured him with hazy smoke and awful fumes, then the beast let out a menacing scream. After a wild fight, he managed to slam the door shut. He then dropped to the ground and started gasping for air. But the room was a disaster. Smoke and ash filled the entire place.

He stayed down on the ground for about five minutes. As he tried catching his breath, he pulled his shirt over his mouth and nose, while watching the ashes fly about. As he started to get up, his boss, manager, and head cremator, Mr. Therman, came in and saw him hunched over.

Mr. Therman said, "What the hell is going on in here?"

Dylan replied, "You wouldn't believe me if I told you."

"Well, lay it on me, I've been doing this for 60 years, I've about seen it all."

"I think this place is tainted. I felt the grip of death grab me on that last body."

"This job does that to you after a while, son. I've seen things here you couldn't even imagine. Well, after the mess here, maybe you can imagine it. But that grip of death is just a reminder that you can sometimes feel dead inside working here. It's just a reminder that you're not dead yet when you feel something."

Then he walked to the burner, opened the door, and stuck his arm inside. He looked back at Dylan and said, "See?" He pulled his arm out and looked at Dylan, "What did I tell you?" Mr. Therman had no pain at all and no burn marks. Dylan was even more frightened. Mr. Therman smiled at him, then he left the room.

He knew right there that Mr. Therman was a ghost or the walking dead. He soon realized that this could be his future. It all made sense to him now. Mr. Therman had been there since he was twenty. He looked way too well to be a man of 80. He looked about 50. He also moved way too well. He was spry and in great shape. It also made sense how he lived on the premises and seemed to never leave. Dylan now believed Mr. Therman was trapped there for eternity.

Dylan decided right then that he would leave that night and never return. He knew if he kept working there, he would be trapped to spend the rest of eternity burning bodies.

He kept working the rest of the day as if nothing had happened. Mr. Therman kept coming in to check on him. Every time he did, Dylan grew cold and nervous. Now that he knew the truth, his body chilled like ice, and even the burning stove couldn't melt or break his chill.

As Dylan was packing up to leave, Mr. Therman came up to him and asked him to come into his office before he left. Dylan made the mistake of doing so. When Dylan entered, he just knew he made the wrong choice. Just an eerie feeling; the eeriest he had felt all day.

Mr. Therman said to him, "Come on in, sit down." Dylan took a seat. Mr. Therman spoke again and said, "I think you know why I asked you to talk." Dylan gulped and shook. "Since you have worked here long enough, I think it is time you help me run this place forever."

"Um, what do you mean by that?"

Mr. Therman's face transformed into that of an awful beast; he had a bright yellow face and awful monstrous teeth. Mr. Therman said to him, "You know exactly what I mean!!!" He spoke in a traitorous raspy voice.

Dylan jumped up and ran to the door, but he was stopped by the standing bare body of a man that was scheduled to be burned the next day. The corpse grabbed onto him. Dylan went completely numb. The ghost pulled him down to the ground while the cold ghostly grip of Mr. Therman grabbed onto him. His numbness faded and he started letting out screams and cries. But the ghost and dead bodies pulled him down the hall to the roasting room.

Dylan tried fighting back, but Mr. Therman grabbed his throat and sent him back to the numb state. When they got him into the room, another dead body was standing waiting at the oven. The corpse had the door opened and the fire blazing. Then, the corpse along with three ghostly creatures latched onto Dylan and dragged him to the oven. They each grabbed a limb and tossed Dylan into the broiler. He let out the most horrid scream, and then one of the corpses slammed the door shut. Then they collapsed, back to their dead form, where they waited to burn the next day.

Dylan died a terrible death, one of the most awful states, being burned alive. The next day, he woke and was thinking it was only a dream. But when he looked around, he soon realized he was not in his own home. It was a room he had never seen before. He stood up and walked out the door. He walked out to a kitchen and living room. He saw Mr. Therman standing at the kitchen counter pouring two cups of coffee. At first, Dylan thought he might still be dreaming.

Mr. Therman told him to come and sit down, so

Dylan did so. Mr. Therman also sat down and then handed him a cup of coffee.

Then Mr. Therman spoke and said, "Well son, sorry we had to do what we did last night. it's just the way life is. As I said, this place gets to you after a while. Now you will really relate to all your clients. You and I will reside here for the rest of eternity, I guess I never showed you the basement. You know what they say when you work at a place long enough, you become that place."

THE TRACKS

An old drifter, or what some would call a bum, was walking down the tracks. He had been walking down the tracks for most of his life since he was a young punk. He had seen it all; he'd jump a train whenever he could or sometimes, he would just walk. He liked walking the tracks, it reminded him of being a kid. Back when he and his friends would travel to get around town. It was always the easiest way to get places quickly and undetected.

Mikey the drifter had many good memories on the tracks when he was young, including drinking underage, buying cigarettes from the homeless, and even a few fights he took part in. A few of the fights were one on one. Some involved him and his friends versus another group of guys they didn't like. He even got jumped walking home one night.

When he was fifteen, he and his buddies were having a party on the tracks; they were so liquored up that they didn't even bother starting a fire. They drank until three in the morning. Slowly they felt the tracks rumble. They had their music very loud, so at first, they couldn't hear much until a loud horn started blaring. The young teens started to realize a train was headed toward them; they all jumped and ran away from the tracks. Unfortunately, the youngest of them, Lenny, didn't know which way he should run, he was so messed up on drugs and alcohol that he kept running on the track until the train crushed him. Lenny's body was destroyed under the train at the young age of fourteen. After that, the boys all went their separate ways. Mikey decided to just keep on walking the tracks. He never went back to live with his parents. The tracks became his new home.

It just became an instinct, something just clicked or maybe even unclicked in his brain. After the tragedy, he spent the entire next day walking. Mikey, the new-found drifter, walked for damn-near forty-eight hours. After two days of walking, that night he looked to his side, and he saw some flames off in the woods. He looked around and he noticed he was farther down the tracks than he had ever been. He didn't know why or how he was that far out? Mikey had lived on the complete instinct to flee for two days. Now that he had seen the light in the forest, he realized he was still alive, and he needed something to eat.

He walked down a path that took him towards the fire where four hobos were cooking some beans and drinking cheap wine.

As Mikey walked towards them, one of the tramps yelled, "Who goes there?"

"My name's Mikey. I seemed to have lost my way."

The tramp yelled back "Aww haven't we all, get the hell out of here!"

Another one of the homeless men butt in and yelled "Don't mind him, he's an arse hole. Come have a seat, friend."

Mikey walked through the woods and made his way to where the four train tramps were enjoying their wine and beans. They asked Mikey if he wanted anything; he obviously took them up on the offer.

He was very thankful for their hospitality.

He told the men he didn't have much memory of what had happened. All he remembered was an awful scream and a horn squeal. His next memory was seeing the fire that he was now sitting by. The last few days for him were a blur.

After a few drinks of wine and some scoops of beans with the tramps, Mikey started to remember what had happened. He told his tale to the winos. As he told them the story, everything went purple. The men started hazing away to nothing. He started walking through the dark mists and he saw his good friend Lenny through the trees. Lenny stopped quickly and waved with a wink, then he was gone in a flash. Mikey didn't know what was going on, all reality had shifted. Finally, it came rushing back, all at once, it hit him like a punch in the gut; he dropped to the ground where he remained for the night. When he woke up in the morning, he saw a bag of goods sitting on the ground beside him next to the burnt-out fire.

Mikey again did not have much memory of the night before. All he really remembered was falling asleep near a fire. The rest of his past life had seemed to be a blur. It now seemed to him that his entire life he was walking the tracks. So, he kept on foot for two more days. Along his way, he kept dreaming of the weird haze and the friendly winos he thought he hallucinated. Every morning he woke up with supplies nearby. He wasn't sure if these were things he dreamed of or if they were real, or maybe if the tracks were just getting to him. After another two days of travelling through pleasant weather through the woods, he came across a town with a station. There were lots of trains coming in and out, heading towards different track systems, this was a junction for them.

Mikey saw a livestock train heading the opposite way from his former home. He kept an eye on it until he saw it was starting to steam up; he snuck onto a hay cart. He knew it would be a long haul because the next farming town was quite a ways away. He travelled through the night on the hay wagon; he was all on his own. He felt very peaceful; he was at ease. Mikey was lying on one bail and leaning against another. Everything seemed normal to him until a man appeared before him. He had a plaid jacket, overalls, a large cowboy hat, and he smoked a pipe.

He sat down across from Mikey, then he said, "Howdy partner."

Mikey was puzzled, but not frightened. He decided he would treat every moment on the tracks as a dream. These encounters were just normal. He soon started jumping on a new train every chance he got, and if he was in a new area he had never seen, he hopped off and went for a walk. He went across the country many times over and over. He encountered many different people. He didn't know how many of them were real and how many were figments of his imagination, or what he sometimes wondered were ghosts. One time, he was speaking with a tramp on a freighter, and Mikey told him about the things he had seen and how he wondered if they were real or not. The fellow tramp told him he had seen many of the same things and he also wondered if they were real or not. He confided to him that he wondered if he himself was even real.

After fifty years on the tracks, Mikey's only reality was the tracks, be it real or fantasy. One day, the elderly train dweller was walking on the top of the carts. Even in his old age, he hadn't fallen off the top. When Mikey got to one of the carts, he saw a gang of teens on the top. They were smoking and drinking around a fire. Mikey went up to the kids and asked for a smoke. He wasn't sure if they were real or just fantasy. Most of the time, people were friendly on the tracks even though he had had a few rough encounters.

As Mikey went up to the kids, one came straight for him and punched him. Another grabbed him by the shoulders and then through him towards the middle of two carts. The kids started beating poor old Mikey. Mikey now realized that this was a reality, the pain he felt had to be real, it was too great not to be. As they beat him, one of the teens grabbed Mikey's weak body and pushed him between two of the carts. Mikey was completely squashed and mangled. His body was completely destroyed. The teens went back to the fire as if nothing had happened.

All of a sudden, a dark cloud with red eyes swarmed towards them; it let out a loud holler, warning them of what was coming. The cloud rushed towards them with a large gust of wind, knocking them off and trapping them under the train, damning their souls to the tracks.

Mikey found himself lying on top of the cart he had just fallen from. As he stood up, he saw Lenny and a few other friends he had met on the tracks.

Lenny called over to him. "Hey Mikey, it's been a

while. Come join us." Mikey went over to his old friends. When he got up to them, Lenny said, "You know, some people are damned to these tracks, but you seem to enjoy it. It looks like you have made a lot of good friends along the way. I think we will all have a good time on these tracks now."

Mikey looked around and didn't think it could get any better, he already thought the tracks were heaven, but now they truly were.

CIVIL ZOMBIES

Ten years after the Civil War, a young outlaw was living in a southern state. He had heard many rumblings of a ghost town within the region. The story goes as follows, the town of Canyon Brook was destroyed during the war, and it is now haunted by the unrested souls of the confederates that died there. The young outlaw, Johnny Thunder, did not believe in such a place. He had been all over the state, especially the nearby counties, searching for it.

Johnny Thunder tried not to stay in the same place for long, but he always ended up finding himself looking for Canyon Brook when he was on

Johnny Thunder tried not to stay in the same place for long, but he always ended up finding himself looking for Canyon Brook when he was on the run. He started getting bored of the hotel he was hiding out in, so he decided it was time to go back on the run.

Johnny Thunder left his room and walked out of the hotel saloon with his hat drawn down and a bandana covering up his face. He jumped on the horse he had been keeping at the bar and rode down to the bank. He hitched his horse with a quick-release knot. Johnny ran into the bank and immediately opened fire. He was a shoot-first-ask-questions later, kind of guy. After shooting the teller, he started demanding money from the rest of them.

He got the money from them quite quickly. And while he didn't drain the bank, he stole enough to get him through to his next job. He didn't want to waste time taking money from the safe, as he knew the sheriff checked in frequently. Sure enough, as he came running outside, the sheriff was waiting for him. The officer fired his gun, but it hit the bank window beside Johnny. This gave Johnny time to fire back and drop the sheriff dead.

Johnny jumped on his horse, pulled the knot loose, and kicked his mount into action. He charged down the main street of town. As he exited the town border, he thought he was free. But when he looked back over his shoulder, he saw what looked to be two deputies and a bounty hunter chasing after him.

At first, Johnny didn't open fire; he didn't want to waste ammo until he needed it. He started heading towards a hill to evade them. A bullet flew right in front of Johnny which spooked the horse, but Johnny got it back under control quickly. Johnny then pulled his .45 and fired three shots at his pursuers. He saw one man fall, heard another scream, and the other man kept riding unharmed. Johnny switched to his other revolver, he wanted to keep two shots in the chambers of both guns.

He fired two shots, but each missed its target. He pushed on and started to lose them up on the hill. He went up a narrow and jagged path. His horse struggled to make it up, but he pushed it on, it was a strong horse. By the time they made it, they had turned around many corners while the remaining deputies were just starting up the trail.

Johnny Thunder stopped at the top, he thought he had outrun them until he could hear bullets going off in a far distance; he knew he hadn't lost them yet. Johnny kept pushing his horse across the highland, knowing he had to keep going.

He kept forward until he realized he was on the top of the cliffs he had been riding along. He could vaguely hear and see the deputies approaching him.

He kept going in the same direction until he came to a large rock that led up another cliff range. He thought about going up but that would leave him as an open target. The angle was too steep, even if he could make it up. Instead, Johnny saw a very narrow ledge just big enough for a horse. Johnny directed the horse down the ledge, it was nerve-racking, but he hoped they would not notice him going down.

The ledge curved diagonally across a large part of the cliff face. By the time the deputies got there, he was tucked away in the rock face. The two law enforcers didn't even notice the trail. The two decided to call it a cold case and they headed home for the day.

Johnny continued downward until he reached the bottom of the canyon. As he arrived at the bottom, he realized he had never been down this trail before. Once he got to the bottom, there was a small river going through the canyon, it led right out through a narrow passage. Halfway through the canyon, and quite a ways away, he saw what looked to be a couple of structures. He rode steadily towards them. When he approached them, he saw a series of abandoned buildings that looked to be a town at one point in history. Johnny realized he had finally found the ghost town of Canyon Brook. Now he realized why that was its name, being along a brook at the bottom of a canyon.

The buildings were half-crisped as it looked as if the whole town was set to blaze. He looked down to the end of the canyon. It looked as if the exit opening had closed in as if there was no escaping the canyon. Johnny decided to stay put for the night, he thought it would be nice to spend the night in such a historical spot. A place he had searched for his whole life. He browsed around, but he didn't see anything that looked to be human remains, although there were signs of dismay. Weapons were scattered everywhere, and Union and confederate uniforms were lying on the ground. Johnny thought it was quite odd to find no bodies amongst all the destruction. He gathered up everything he could as he inspected the area, everything he thought was valuable or useful. Mainly some scattered weaponry, and a few pieces of jewelry, there was not much left. All the food and alcohol were completely gone.

He thought that maybe someone had cleaned out the town and taken all the bodies with them, but that didn't make sense. Why there would still be uniforms and weapons?

Once it started getting too dark for comfort, Johnny sat down on his bedroll. He grew quite cold, being in the canyon overnight. He was unable to sleep at first; he had a lot on his mind, being in a historic town that was completely deserted with nothing but weapons and uniforms. After some hesitation, he shut his mind down and fell asleep.

He dreamed of fighting in the civil war. He saw his face on both sides of the battlefield, shooting at himself. One of his bodies dropped to the ground, then he got up with his flesh turning dark and deteriorated. His dead form walked over to his other self. The living version kept firing at his walking dead body. But the zombie kept moving and took him down. Just as the dream got to its peak, a loud burst of thunder rolled in. Johnny jumped awake.

He looked around and saw that it was all a dream. He was still in the abandoned ghost town, at least he thought it was abandoned.

He started to doze back to sleep when he heard the fire of a gun and some screaming. He couldn't make out what the men were saying, it was just a bunch of loud terrible screams. Soon more gunfire started; it was coming from different directions. At the same time, a storm rolled in, the hard thunder got louder, and the rain came pouring down. The horse had not run off, yet and Johnny was very thankful for this. He grabbed his bag of guns and ammunition and jumped on his high-quality lifted mount. He started riding away from the ghost town until he saw about forty union soldiers coming toward him. They were all rotting corpses of the soldiers they once were. But they wielded their weapons strong and fired directly at Johnny. Johnny Thunder turned his horse and stormed away from them; the rain fell hard on him. The zombie soldiers had a hard time keeping up with him, them being dead and all.

He thought he had gotten away from them until he realized he had somehow circled right back toward the town. Waiting for him were at least fifty rebel troops standing guard. Johnny realized he was now in the civil war and had no help, it was only him, and his hope to get the hell out of there to tell a tale that no one would ever believe.

He rode down the middle of the two armies, trying to get away from them, but bullets started to fire between the two. He didn't want to risk his horse; he would need it after his fight with the two sides. Once Johnny got to a half-dilapidated structure, he steered the horse behind it and then jumped off with his bag of guns. He settled into an optimal yet comfortable position, then he opened fire. He started picking off soldiers on both sides with ease. At first, it seemed too easy for him. Horses began to rise from the ground where the soldiers were standing. When he shot a soldier down it would get right back up, he was wasting ammunition. Once the zombie horses had all risen from the ground, Johnny knew his luck might be running slim. Then it got even worse. Soldiers were coming out of the canyon walls. One fired a shot right by his horse. Johnny jumped back on as it was now spooked, and he needed to calm it down for he now knew how to get out of there.

He hoped he could get right through the union line without them noticing. His plan was that the thunder and lightning and the raining bullets would be enough to distract them long enough for him to get through.

He charged through the storm. He grabbed the .45 magnums he was wielding and fired them stunning the zombies long enough to get through their line; some fell right off their horses. He got past the line, but it wasn't the end. His new goal was to get to the end of the canyon along the river brook, if that was even possible, with a torrential storm hammering in. The zombies were not his major concern anymore. The union army had quickly defeated the rebel and was now coming after him. With the union army after him and sharpshooters on the cliff, plus rocks crumbling from the surrounding canyon walls, it couldn't get any worse. Then the sharpshooters started to fall to the ground as the entire canyon started to cave in on itself.

The thunder roared and Johnny and his horse were going on complete adrenaline. He had a great distance from the zombies. The union horses weren't moving as fast as his lively steed. He looked back to see where they were, but as he looked the rocks continued to fall and the ground started sinking in around him. This made Johnny's horse go even faster as it knew this could be the end for them both.

As they neared the end of the trail, they were

dodging rocks. Johnny could see the very narrow exit between the river and the rock walls. He finally reached the end. He believed he had made it until a huge rock began to crumble down, it was about to block the only way out just a few feet in front of him. As he was about to make a jump for it, the horse stumbled downward. Johnny leaped off the horse as it went down, he was able to fly over the gap with the momentum.

He was thrown from his horse, landing on his stomach just on the other side of the fallen rock that now blocked any way out. The rock stood over six feet tall. The storm slowed down after having escaped out of the tunnel; it was just a light rain now. Johnny was completely relieved being out, despite feeling dazed, the relief was the stronger emotion.

Then he realized his mount hadn't made it through the narrow gap and had been left behind. He stood looking at the large tomb, then lowered his hat with a moment of silence. As he looked down with his eye closed, he heard a loud neigh. He looked up with disbelief, his beautiful horse gracefully leaped over the large rock. His horse looked alive and well and thankfully didn't look like a zombie. It was the happiest moment he could remember having in a long time. When the horse ran right to him, he jumped on.

As he sat on his mount, he thought to himself, well, I guess I'm off to the next town. Maybe I can fool some sucker into believing this. I guess I'll have to find a new legend to discover, maybe I can get a witness next time. He grabbed an apple from his saddle bag as he rode in the light rain. He then stopped his mount, leaned over, and gave it the apple. Then he gave it a good pat on the back before they set off again on a new adventure.

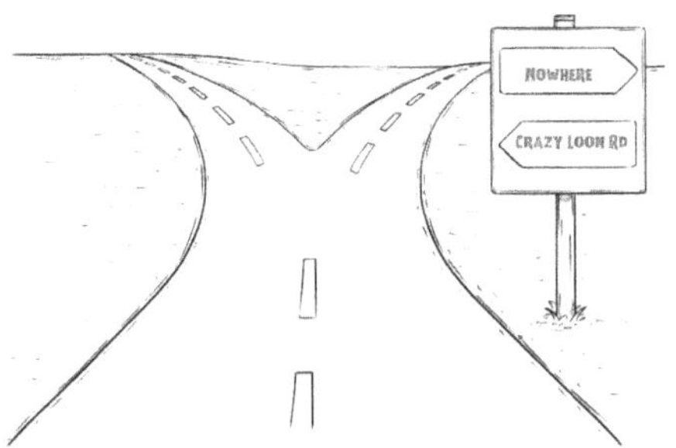

CRAZY LOON ROAD

itch Guthrie was thirty-four; he was on his way to a cottage he had just inherited from his great-uncle. He was driving an eighty-nine Chevy pickup with a canoe attached across the bed and roof. His truck had a lot of rust on it; he couldn't believe a Chev had made it that long. He wished his uncle had left him his Ram, but he was still excited about the cottage. He had never been to it before. It was his first time driving down these winding roads. He started out down a flat straight highway through some farming land. It didn't even look like there was water nearby. He drove down the highway passing corn fields, apple orchards, and some cattle.

After a few hours, he drove past the road he was looking for, it was called Crazy Loon Road. Mitch always thought it was a funny name for a road. He figured there were a lot of loons by the water and some crazy drunks to go with it, like every part of cottage country.

Mitch turned the truck around. Crazy Loon Road was very curvy with lots of trees. The forest was thick with branches popping out and smacking the canoe and his windshield. He was scared it was going to fall off. After ten minutes of driving, he hadn't seen any signs of life except some bugs. That was until a bear walked down the road straight towards him. Mitch started to get somewhat nervous as it got closer and pulled his truck to the side of the road. Mitch had only seen bears far out in the water across a lake or large river. He wasn't sure what the bear was going to do until it faded to the left into the brush. Mitch put the truck back in gear and started down the road. He drove down this road for an hour until it finally started to open up. It was still thick with vegetation, but it looked like there could be a sign of human activity. He drove down the wide road for a few more minutes, then he came to the end of the road which led him into a driveway beside a large two-story cottage.

Mitch was very surprised to see that this was the only home on such a large road. He was now questioning why it was named Crazy Loon Road. He hurried to the cottage with his things as he didn't want to stay out too long with the bears running wild. As he walked into the cottage, he could hear many loons in the distant wild. He loved the sound; it sounded like they were singing as a choir.

Inside the cottage, he noticed there were many guns across the walls, along with stuffed animals, including fish and stuffed bears standing in the front room. He even had a stuffed loon with its wings spread open and suspended from the ceiling. He didn't realize how big of a hunter his uncle was. He also didn't know you could hunt loons. There were plenty of them throughout the house. He realized his uncle was the crazy loon for killing such a beautiful animal. He could still hear their song even from inside the cottage. He decided he would take his canoe out for a late-night trip and explore the surrounding water. He wanted to be out with the loons in the cold dark night. He wasn't too worried about the bears; but to be safe, he brought his uncle's shotgun with him.

He took the canoe out to the water; he could hear the loons growing stronger, but when he got to the edges of the water, he could not see any of the beautiful birds. He paddled out of the bay where his dock was and made his way to the dark open lake. When he got out there, he decided he would throw out a few casts on his fishing rod. He didn't feel any bites at first; he started reeling his line in slowly hoping to get some attention. As he started to reel, he saw two dark red eyes glaring at him just above the surface of the dark lake. He laid his eyes on it for a second, and then it was gone. As it disappeared, a loud call of a loon cried out before he got a huge bite on his rod. It tugged his line so hard that his boat began to tip. Then the beast on the other end of the line flew up and started shaking the boat. He could see that it was a loon. It was holding tight to his line, and it ripped the rod out of Mitch's hand. Without hesitating, the red-eyed beast flew towards him.

Mitch had no choice but to pull out his uncle's shotgun and kill the frightening, yet beautiful bird. He fired two shells from the double barrel. The bird let out an awful cry and dropped into the lake. Mitch started to paddle back to the cottage, the loud sound of loons surrounded him, though he could not see them. He just kept paddling until he could see the light of the cottage nearby. Mitch thought he was about to make it back until five large loons rose from the water and completely flipped the boat upright until it was upside down in the water.

Mitch lost the shotgun he was holding, but he still had a pistol in his pocket. He reached for it and fired at the birds. All he could see were red eyes coming at him and knocking him down. One of the loons picked him up and carried him to the land. It pecked at him while the rest came over and surrounded him. As he thought the awful bird was about to kill him, the face of his great-uncle appeared.

"Hey kid, I bet you thought you were lucky when I gave you this place. Truth is, I never liked you. I always thought you were a spoiled rotten brat. So, I left you an old hunting shack that was taken over by mad loons a few years back. Well, here you go, kid.

You get what you deserve."

The loons all let out a shrill call. Mitch's screams were soon muffled by the loud yet beautifully mad birds.

CAT HOUSE

There was once a century-old house. It was covered in vines and moss with a large yard in front of it. The front yard was full of shrubs that had started to fill in the walkway that led to the vine-covered door. Before the front door rested a balcony that didn't look like it had been opened in ages. Nicholas had just moved in across the street with his mother and brother. He was 12 and his younger brother Bobby, was eight. Nicholas and Bobby liked to have a lot of adventures. Nicholas had looked across to this house every day for the last month. He was really starting to wonder about it. He never saw anyone leave, and the only sign of life were the cats that always looted around the front yard, sidewalk, and even the street. There were always at least three cats out there, sometimes even four or five.

The boys were on summer vacation; they liked skateboarding on the street outside their house. It was a Tuesday afternoon. Their grandmother was supposed to be watching them while their mother was at work, but she was mainly watching soap operas in the living room. The boys didn't need anyone taking care of them, but they liked getting into trouble, so it was always a good idea to have someone there. As the boys had not gotten into any trouble since living there, their grandmother had really gotten into watching her soap operas. Her favourite was something about a witch and a doll.

While the boys were out skateboarding on the road, another kid about ten years old came towards them riding his scooter down the street.

When he got up to them, he introduced himself as Timothy. Then he said, "So, you guys are the lucky ones that got to move across from a haunted house."

"What are you talking about?" Nicholas replied.

"You haven't heard? That house has been haunted for the last year. An old lady died there a year ago. She had two cats, but since her death, there are at least half a dozen. I think the whole house is full of them now. Apparently, they ate her."

Nicholas and Bobby stared at each other for a split moment; their jaws dropped. Then Nicholas replied, "You're full of it."

"Whatever, have fun living across from a ghost house. If you don't believe me, maybe you should go in and tell me if I'm wrong."

Nicholas and Bobby both knew they had to go in there now. Neither one of them could turn down a challenge. Then Bobby spoke up and said, "You're on butt head!"

Then Nicholas added, "Yeah, we'll go in there, but only because you're obviously too chicken to do so."

"I'm not chicken," Timothy said with attitude.

"If you're not, then come with us tonight at midnight."

"Fine, I'll be here, you turd munchers."

"Okay, see you tonight. Now get away from us, jerk"

The kid turned around on his scooter and as he left, he gave them a nice friendly middle finger.

Nicholas and Tommy skateboarded the rest of the

day until it got dark. They kept noticing the weird cats. One was a large white cat, very fat; it almost looked mutated. There was a typical black cat in the middle of the walkway and another black cat on the porch, and lastly, they noticed a striped brown one rolling on its back in the street. Many of the cats gave them awful stares. Once it hit eight o'clock and the darkness started to approach the two boys got scared. The creepy cats all sat beside each other on the sidewalk blocking the walkway to the door. The scary white one even gave them an awful hiss showing its teeth. At the same time, they noticed the drapes moving in the window upstairs. It looked as if there was a figure passing by. They also saw what they thought was a pair of red eyes peering through.

They looked at each other and gulped. They both were thinking the same thing, that they might have bitten off more than they could chew.

Bobby said to Nicholas, "There's no way cats could eat a person? Is there?"

Nicholas replied unsurely, "No that can't be true."

"Do you think anybody could be living in there?"

"No, that's impossible. Let's go inside for supper."

The boys cooked up a frozen pizza while their mother watched TV on the couch and rested. She went to bed an hour later, and the boys waited up in Nicholas's room staring out at the house they were getting ready to enter.

They stared out the window the entire time not saying too much to each other; their nerves taking them over. They were both hoping that Timothy wouldn't show up. This was the first adventure they did not feel up for. Despite them hoping he wouldn't show, he was there at 12:01. Timothy saw them staring out Nicholas's window. He waved them to come out and picked up a stone and got ready to throw it until they open the window and climbed out.

Timothy said, "What's keeping you guys? Let's go."

The boys hurried over to him. The three snuck over to the yard across the street and hid in the well-overgrown bush. They sat for a moment, getting their plans ready when they heard something in the bush. It got each of their attention. A cat jumped out in front of them and let out an awful cry with its claw up and ready to swipe; it had awful teeth. This was an orange cat they had never seen before. Timothy and Bobby were very startled by this.

Nicholas laughed at both of them and then shushed them before he said, "Quiet. Let's go to the backyard. I see a gate over there."

The three of them walked through the bushy yard. They could hear cats whining, purring, and hissing, but they could not see any. No more popped out into their path. Once they got to the gate, they busted it open with one push. Pressing forward, they saw a large backyard; it was full of knee-high grass, very easy for cats to hide in. The three walked slowly through the tall grass. Nicholas led the way, each of them was terrified. It got even worse for them when they noticed the first back door was partially opened.

It was a white door, most of the paint was chipped off and it didn't look like there was much keeping it together. A large gust of wind came in and the door blew open, Nicholas kept going, but the younger boys stopped in their tracks.

Nicholas said to them, "Come on guys, don't chicken out now. We have to go inside; we've made it this far." Nicholas seemed to have grown a much bigger spine just walking through the front yard and gate. It was the natural adventurer in him.

Bobby replied, "Yeah, let's go." He started

walking and Timothy still stood dead in his tracks. Then Bobby said to him. "Come on chicken, this was your idea, tough guy."

Timothy cringed and followed behind them without saying a word. Nicholas went in first. When the three of them were all past the first door, they noticed that they were in an old tool shed attached to the house. As they went to open the door to the main part of the house, a cat came walking right through the door. Timothy and Bobby each let out an awful gasp. Nicholas even stepped back a bit in fright.

They all thought it was a ghost until Nicholas realized there was a cat door.

He said to them, "See guys, there's a door." The cat brushed against his leg looking for some attention. Nicholas patted it on the head and commented, "See guys, it's friendly. Let's keep going."

But Timothy was already starting to walk away. Then Bobby said, "You're not going anywhere. You got us in here, you're coming too."

Timothy still didn't like it, he said, "Let's just go, we made it inside, now we can go."

Nicholas replied to Timothy, "We agreed to see if it was haunted; we haven't figured that out yet.

So, you're coming with us even if I have to force you."

"Okay, okay. Just relax, I'm coming."

Then the friendly cat sat in front of him and let out a soft meow. Timothy let out an "eek!" at the friendly kitty, Bobby and Nicholas both laughed and started their way into the home. When they got inside, they noticed it was filled with cat toys and, of course, many cats. There was a dozen elaborate scratching posts scattered around with cats on top of them relaxing. The kitchen was filled with them too.

As they made their way in, some of the cats made awful hisses, but others came up to them purring and rubbing their legs like the other one. When they got halfway through the living room, they saw a stairway to the basement and another to the upstairs. They weren't sure which to explore first until they saw a large cat carrying a rat up the stairs and run with it over to the bottom of the upstairs stairwell. It obviously was feeding kittens under there. The basement was where they got their food supply.

Nicholas decided to lead the boys up the stairs, he figured rats would be an adventure for another night.

Nicholas started walking up the stairs, he wanted

to see what was in the room where he had seen the figure from outside. Once they got up the stairs, it was the first room in front of them. Bobby walked at the back of the line so Timothy couldn't turn and leave. As Nicholas walked along the second level toward the door, they could hear creaking; they figured it was the cats. They could see a few up there, even though it was dark. Before Nicholas opened the door, he saw a small antique table with a document on top. He picked it up and opened it. It was a will saying that the house was to be left to the city as a cat sanctuary. There was a picture of an elderly woman on it; it read, in loving memory of Nadine Coons, who died of old age in the local hospital. This will remain a home for her pets, all cats are welcome.

Nicholas said to Timothy, "See, she didn't get eaten by cats at all, you liar."

Timothy nervously laughed, "Ha, and you believed me! Now, let's get out of here." Timothy then tried turning around but Bobby stopped him even though he was younger; he was tougher and much braver than Timothy.

Nicholas said, "We'll open this door, and then we can go."

Nicholas creaked open the door. As he opened it all

the way, they heard chirps. They walked a little farther in. Once Nicholas got in, followed by Bobby, and Timothy right behind, they were swarmed by bats from all directions. Timothy screamed like a girl, and so did the rest of them. Nicholas started swinging his arms all over, the flying beasts were smacking them with their wings, trying to bite them.

They all fell to the ground. The bats were ready to take their lives. At first, they thought they were dead until they heard a loud roar of a beast. A huge flash of a tiger illuminated the entire place, then it roared until the bats flew away. The room was soon cleared of the bats, many of which went into the walls hiding from the ferocious beast.

They scanned the room for a way to escape, their eyes locating a small window that they could climb out of. As the beast roared, Nicholas jumped up and yelled, "We gotta get outta here!" Timothy and Bobby were both petrified crouching down on the ground. Nicholas grabbed both by the arm and dragged them to their feet and yelled, "Come on," again. This time they were alerted, the tiger still frightened them but now the adrenaline was coursing through their veins. They ran through the bat-infested room out the window towards the balcony.

Although they each got there very quickly all three of them were now stuck on the 20-foot-high balcony. They didn't know what to do. The bats were starting to come at them again.

Nicholas pushed both boys towards the edge of the railing and said, "Climb down guys, I'll fight them off. Bobby and Timothy did what he said and climbed down. Once they got halfway down and there was room for him to climb, he went down too. As the other two were on the ground, he was still 10 feet up. He thought he was in the clear until a swarm of bats flew down on him causing him to lose his grip. He fell to the ground and let out an awful cry. He swiftly jumped to his feet, but he was in severe pain. He could not move his arm at all, but he started to run away despite the pain. Timothy jumped on his scooter and high-tailed it. Once he got halfway across the street the light came on in the brother's house.

Their mother came running out and yelled, "What the hell is going on out here? Get inside!" They went in while their mother scolded them. Nicholas told her he had a lot of pain, and he couldn't move his arm. At first, she was going to make him sit in pain all night but then after an hour, she decided to take him to the hospital. They were there until early morning. Nicholas had a dislocated collar bone and each of them got a rabies shot.

Timothy never told his parents about that night, so he never got a rabies shot. It just so happened they never saw Timothy again. They always just figured he didn't have the guts to be around them. Then, a few months later, they heard of some strange murders, and animal attacks, mostly dogs and livestock. Nicholas started thinking that Timothy might have something to do with it, but he figured he was being over-imaginative. He just wanted to believe it so he could make an adventure out of finding out the truth.

FRIENDS 'TILL THE END

On a nice winter day, a family, which consisted of a mother, father, and their son, moved to a new town into an old house. The house was in a very ritzy, historic part of town with other very beautiful old houses. They unpacked and settled in, thinking how great it was to be in such an old, historic house. Sometimes, they would get a chill walking from one room to another, but the father of the family just assumed it was because it was an old house and had a draft. He started thinking of ways to fix it.

One day the boy of the house, Billy, was up in his room playing with dinky cars. Then a young boy, about his age, appeared from nowhere and startled him.

Billy exclaimed, "Who are you, where did you come from?"

"Don't worry, my friend. I'm Tommy, I have lived here for a century."

Billy's face went white, and he gasped, "So, you-you-you're a ghost?!"

"Yup, you got it, pal, but don't worry, I'm friendly."

"Really?"

"Yeah, we can be pals. Do you have any friends?"

"No, I'm new to town."

"I thought so. Let's play."

Billy and the ghost played in his room for hours until his parents came in. He was so excited to tell them about his new friend, but when he told them, they did not see Tommy sitting there. They just thought, oh, that's great, our son has a good imagination.

The next day, Billy was outside making an ice rink. He was talking with Tommy the whole time. From his parents' point of view, it looked like he was talking to thin air. They started to think he was getting a little carried away with his imaginary friend. Billy and his ghost friend played for weeks.

Tommy even followed Billy to school. It started to become a problem when he was laughing with Tommy in the classroom. His parents began to get calls from the school, they were suggesting they send him to a psychiatric boarding school; That was the last thing they wanted to do.

Then one day, a kid was calling Billy a freak for seeing a ghost. When the kid turned around and started walking away, Tommy the ghost picked up a baseball bat that was nearby and threw it across the field hitting the kid. The bully came charging towards Billy in retaliation. But when he reached Billy, Tommy stepped in and threw the kid's face toward the ground which completely knocked the wind out of him. Billy got blamed for this. No one saw the bat come out of nowhere, and since the bully was so close to Billy, it looked like he had knocked him down. The bully thought so too.

The teacher on duty took Billy to the principal's office who called his parents in. They had a big argument about whether ghosts were real or not. Billy told them that Tommy thought they were all idiots. The principal told Billy's parents they had to send him to the psychiatric school program.

Billy ended up getting shipped off to the boarding school. When he got there, he was treated brutally, and he was forced to believe there was no such thing as ghosts. But despite the school's efforts, it would never break Billy. Tommy was with him the whole time.

Billy never ended up leaving the program. He started acting out after enduring their treatment, so they locked him in a padded room to spend the rest of his life. It did not bother Billy because he had his friend Tommy with him the whole time. Tommy would go find out what was happening in the world and tell Billy all the news. Billy enjoyed his time there. It ended up being a place where he could enjoy his life with his best friend.

Eventually, Billy grew old, but since Tommy was a ghost, he remained in the form of a child forever. Sadly, Billy ended up dying in the padded room and his spirit crossed over.

This made Tommy very sad, almost as sad as when he had died. Tommy went back to the house where he died in the first place. He waited for years until a new boy moved in and he could make a new friend to play with.